"You're not free to marry again."

The goading amusement in Lane's tone was too much for Jenna, and her chin lifted rebelliously. "Then I'll just have to instigate divorce proceedings, won't I?"

"I wouldn't recommend it," he drawled.

"Why not?"

"Because I'll fight it. *I'm* quite content with matters the way they are."

"Well, that's just great for you, isn't it?" Jenna flared. "It may come as a shock to you, but I intend to marry Kent, and there's nothing you can do to stop me from getting a judgment on the grounds of separation. We've lived apart for the required number of years."

"Except that I'd have to be agreeable," Lane murmured. "And I'm not. You're my wife, Jenna, and I still consider you as such. There will be no divorce."

Books by Kerry Allyne

HARLEQUIN PRESENTS

HARLEQUIN ROMANCES

These books may be available at your local bookseller.

For a list of all titles currently available,
send your name and address to:

Harlequin Reader Service
P.O. Box 52040, Phoenix, AZ 85072-2040
Canadian address: P.O. Box 2800, Postal Station A,
5170 Yonge St., Willowdale, Ont. M2N 5T5

KERRY ALLYNE

legally bound

Harlequin Books

TORONTO • NEW YORK • LONDON
AMSTERDAM • PARIS • SYDNEY • HAMBURG
STOCKHOLM • ATHENS • TOKYO • MILAN

Harlequin Presents first edition December 1984
ISBN 0-373-10743-9

Original hardcover edition published in 1984
by Mills & Boon Limited

CHAPTER ONE

'HI! How did your holidays go?' enquired Freda Sewell, the chief secretary at Hodgson Industries, of Jenna Bowman on her first day back at work.

Looking tanned and relaxed, her light brown, shoulder length hair even more sun-streaked than usual, Jenna gave a mock rueful smile. 'All too quickly, I'm afraid, although they were certainly enjoyable. Not that I really went anywhere in particular, apart from a week's visit with Mum and Dad up in the mountains. The rest of the time I mainly spent lazing around on the beach every day.'

'So I gathered,' Freda laughed, casting the younger girl's darkly golden skin a wryly envious look. Her own paler than pale skin tones made the beach virtually taboo where she was concerned. 'But I'm sure glad to see you back, and looking so fit and refreshed, because we've been up to our ears in paperwork this last couple of weeks,' she paused, her expression becoming speculative; 'I suppose Kent's already told you there's a take-over of the firm in the pipeline?'

Kent Sharman was the Hodgson's sales representative whom Jenna had been dating for the last six months. 'Yes, as a matter of fact he did tell me there were strong rumours to that effect flying around just after the first week of my holidays,' she nodded as she removed the cover from her typewriter. Her smoky grey eyes rose to the other girl's pleasantly rounded face interestedly, 'So it's definite now, is it?'

'As far as I can tell,' Freda advised, shrugging. 'Everything's still very hush-hush, and old man Hodgson is definitely playing it pretty close to his chest, but Mr Morris,' she named the Works Manager who was also her boss, 'was dropping hints the other day that he might be retiring a few months earlier than he planned because he was too old a dog to be learning new tricks at such a late stage. But that's as much as I've been able to get out of him.'

Which was unusual enough in itself, Jenna mused. Under normal circumstances, Tom Morris kept no business information whatsoever from his extremely trustworthy secretary. 'Not even the name of the firm that's interested in taking us over?' she probed.

Freda shook her head. 'Not so much as a whisper,' she relayed in obviously disappointed tones. 'Although from words picked up here and there I've got my own suspicions that it could be quite a large concern, and that being the case, I guess it could also mean a promotion for your boss, especially if Mr Morris does retire.'

A position Jenna did not doubt Ian Leonard was fully qualified to fill, but, at the same time . . . 'Unless, of course, if this firm is as big as you suspect, they decide to replace Mr Morris with one of their own staff instead. Or even others presently employed here as well, if it comes to that,' she surmised with the beginnings of a frown marring her forehead. With jobs so difficult to come by these days, now was not an auspicious time to suddenly find oneself out of work. 'After all,' she continued in a thoughtful vein, 'as everyone knows, it's been something of a struggle for

Hodgson's to keep going this last couple of years, so I suppose it would be quite within the realms of possibility for them to want to replace and or, at least reduce some of the staff here in order to get the company's finances heading in the right direction again, wouldn't it?'

'Mm, you could have a point,' Freda conceded slowly, reluctantly. Then grimaced. 'With mine the first position on the line I expect, once Mr Morris has gone.'

'Oh, I shouldn't think so,' Jenna was quick to reassure her. 'You've been here the longest, and you know every office procedure backwards. Besides, if Ian does become Works Manager you'll undoubtedly be his secretary—which means, of course . . .' she uttered a rather hollow half laugh, 'that I'm more likely to be the one considered superfluous to the organisation . . . not you.'

Freda's fair brows drew together sharply, 'But they would have to appoint another Projects Manager in Ian's place, surely. I mean, we've always had one.'

'Maybe.' Jenna's soft mouth curved wryly. 'And maybe whoever's bidding for the company has one of their own too . . . complete with secretary already.'

'Well, even if that was the case, I can't imagine them letting you go. You're too good at your work,' declared Freda, briskly encouraging. 'In any event, it's all supposition at this stage, anyway. For all we know the takeover may never eventuate, and we'll have had this depressing conversation for nothing.'

For the sake of her own peace of mind Jenna was inclined to agree, and as the office gradually filled with her fellow workers and she was called upon to answer more enquiries regarding her vacation, she made a concerted effort to dismiss the worrying matter from her thoughts.

Nevertheless, the moment the fatherly figure of her boss appeared, and he shortly thereafter called her into his office for some dictation, the subject promptly resurfaced again; and she took the seat on the opposite side of the leather-topped desk in a somewhat preoccupied manner.

'I hope that look on your face isn't a reflection of your feelings at being back working for me again,' Ian Leonard interrupted her reverie on a joking note.

'What? Oh, no, of course not,' she denied, recovering and giving him a wide smile. In truth, and as he was well aware, she had thoroughly enjoyed working for him for the past three years. How could she not have done when he was probably the most considerate and even-tempered man for whom she had ever worked?

'Then what is the trouble? You and Kent had a few hasty words?' he hazarded banteringly, knowing of her relationship with the younger man.

'No, nothing like that,' Jenna shook her head and smiled again. Only the upward curve of her lips was not quite so pronounced this time, nor did it remain in place quite so long as she unconsciously began chewing at her lower lip. 'It's just this proposed acquisition of the firm that Freda was telling me about earlier. Will it really happen, do you think, Ian?' Her thickly lashed eyes sought his anxiously.

'Oh, yes, it's a goer all right,' he confirmed. Leaning forward slightly, his forearms resting on the desk top, he peered at her closely: 'Although I can't see why that should have caused you any worry.'

'Well, it's not uncommon for jobs to be lost in such circumstances, is it?' She shrugged diffidently.

'And you think yours might be one of them?' His expression was one of total surprise.

Jenna made a vague movement with her hands, 'I—well—it's a distinct possibility, isn't it, if you should become Works Manager when Mr Morris retires? You won't need two secretaries, and if this firm that's taking over doesn't choose to appoint someone to replace you, that could sort of make me somewhat redundant,' she partly laughed, partly grimaced.

'Except that no matter who the next Works Manager's secretary might be, if any heads are going to roll I can think of quite a number that will do so before either yours or Freda's does, believe me!' he advised in ironic accents. 'In any case, a company as progressive and successful as Forrester Electronics didn't get where it is today by disposing of their most proficient staff. They prefer to expand in order to make full use of them.'

There was only a second or two for Jenna to appreciate his first reassuring remark before his second hit her like a thunderbolt and every scrap of colour drained from her face. 'Wh-who did you say?' she just managed to force out in a constricted voice.

'Forrester Electronics,' Ian repeated obligingly. 'You must have heard of them. They're one of the largest distributors of electronic components along the east coast!'

Jenna nodded weakly, thankful that the sun, streaming so brilliantly through the office window beside her, was at least partially shading her face as she strove frantically to regain some composure. 'And that's who will be—will be our head company, is it?' She still could not altogether keep her voice from shaking.

'Mmm, that's right,' came the casual verification that had the churning feeling in her stomach increasing. 'Everything's been kept under very close wraps until now, but as the last of the documents were finalised and duly signed last night I don't suppose it will matter you knowing. It will probably be common knowledge in a day or two anyway.' Halting, he sent her a comforting smile. 'So as I said, with a firm like that I very much doubt you need have any fears about losing your position.'

Oh, God, if he only knew! she despaired, even as she made a supreme effort to appear at least outwardly cheered by his words. If she had thought her job may have been in jeopardy before, it was nothing compared to the danger she knew it to be in now!

Not that she had ever told anyone in the office, apart from Kent, but she had been married at eighteen—and to none other than Lane Forrester, the owner, the brains, and the driving force behind Forrester Electronics. Was still married to him, in fact! she recalled almost hysterically, despite their having been separated for the last five years—although that piece of information, as well as her husband's name, she had not seen fit to divulge, even to Kent. But their parting had not been an amicable one, quite the opposite really; the memory returned to haunt her, and for that reason alone, if for no other, she surmised that the day Lane discovered her name on his payroll would undoubtedly be her last with the company.

With even more disturbing thoughts to occupy her mind now than when she had first entered the office, how she managed to take down Ian's dictation that morning Jenna never knew! Although, since her shorthand was the result of an automatic action rather than an attentive one, she really was not at all surprised when she experienced some difficulty in transcribing her notes later.

An occurrence that had her wondering if she would not be better disposed to resign immediately rather than wait meekly for the worst to eventuate, but as it was such a happy office and everyone worked in so well together—notwithstanding having absolutely no idea how she could possibly explain such a precipitate action satisfactorily to Kent without disclosing the truth—she finally dismissed the idea. After all, why should she be forced into leaving? She liked it here, and surely it was doubtful if Lane himself would be conducting the take-over? His firm was certainly large enough now for him to have others doing that kind of work for him; and even if he did take a hand it was still highly improbable that he would show any interest in his newly acquired, but lowly, secretaries, wasn't it?

During the next two weeks various members of the Forrester organisation made visits to the Hodgson office and manufacturing plant, but as Lane wasn't among them Jenna gradually felt able to relax once more, and be pleased that she had not allowed herself to be stampeded into resigning.

'It's nice to see you back to normal again,' even Kent commented as he saw her to the door of her small flat in Burwood, one of Sydney's western suburbs, after an evening at the city's new Entertainment Centre. 'You seem to have been very distant and preoccupied since returning from holidays.'

'Have I?' she countered lightly, pretending not to

have realised. 'I'm sorry, I didn't mean to be.' Opening her front door, she went on quickly. 'How about a cup of coffee before you go?'

He gave a slight shake of his fair head. 'No, I'd better not, thanks all the same. It's late and I've still got to get through all that city traffic again to reach my place. Besides,' his voice thickened as he caught her to him possessively, 'it's hard enough saying goodnight to you here, without doing it in sight of your bedroom!' With a groan he lowered his mouth to hers, his breathing becoming increasingly heavy as she responded. 'For God's sake, Jenna, why won't you marry me?' he pleaded hoarsely against her soft lips. 'You know how I feel about you, how much I want you!'

Easing away from him as far as his arms would permit, Jenna discomfitedly averted her gaze, 'And you know how I feel about marriage,' she murmured in deprecating tones. 'I'm sorry, Kent, but once was enough.'

'But you were only eighteen then! Hardly old enough to know what marriage entailed!' he defended earnestly. 'You're twenty-five now, though, and it's a whole new ball game. Just because your first marriage went on the rocks, doesn't mean ours would too.'

'I know,' she sighed miserably as feelings of guilt swamped her. She really should have told him the whole truth at the beginning of their relationship, she supposed, but even after so many years the emotions evoked by just talking about her marriage were so powerful, and so distressing, that she could still only touch on the subject in the briefest possible manner. At the time it had just never occurred to her that her association with Kent would last so long. Certainly none of the few other men she had dated since leaving Lane had succeeded in seeing her more than a couple of times. She sighed again, smiling half-apologetically, 'It's just that I don't really feel I'm ready to try again yet.'

'Or you don't love me enough to want to?' he deduced on a disappointed note.

These days Jenna was not sure she even knew what love was. She had believed she did once, but now . . . She liked Kent, liked him a lot, but as she knew only too well, that was a far cry from actually loving someone. 'Let's just say I'm wary of ever again committing myself totally,' she compromised.

'Oh, Jen . . . Jen!' He shook his head despairingly. 'You make it tough on a guy, you really do. But I'm not giving up.' His voice strengthened resolutely. 'I'll have you agreeing with me yet, you see if I don't.'

'Perhaps you will, at that,' she smiled encouragingly. It would definitely make things easier if he could. Then she would have no reservations at all about telling him she was only separated, and not divorced as he believed—and would finally provide her with a strong enough reason to subject herself to the sometimes turbulent, but always costly, procedure that would eliminate the last tie that kept her legally bound to Lane.

'Well, I sure hope it's soon. I don't think I can wait much longer,' Kent declared on a roughening note as he threaded his fingers within the sun-brightened strands of her hair. 'You're very tempting, you know, and at moments like this all I can think about is making love to you,' he paused, his eyes holding hers half pleading, half joking. 'I don't suppose you'd consider moving in with me while you're making up your mind?'

With a wry curve catching at her mouth, Jenna gave a negative shake of her head. 'You already know my answer to that.'

'Yeah, I know.' He expelled a heavily resigned breath. 'That's probably one of the reasons why I want you so much. I know you're not the type that sleeps around. Still, it was worth another try,' he smiled crookedly, and planted a lingering kiss to her parted lips. 'In the meantime, though, it's not getting any earlier, and I guess it wouldn't do to be late for work the first day under the new regime, so I expect I'd best be on my way.' Releasing her reluctantly, he took a step towards the stairs leading down to the building's entrance.

'That's right, tomorrow's the big day when we officially become employees of Forrester Electronics, isn't it?' She could not keep a tinge of sardonic ascerbity out of her voice, although thankfully Kent did not appear to notice it.

'Sure is,' he nodded. 'And I must admit that I, for one, am looking forward to it. I was speaking to their Sales Manager when he came to inspect our set-up last week, and from what he had to say I think it's going to be a pleasure working for such a go-ahead company. There's certainly no vacillating among their executives as to which lines will be sellers and which won't. Not like there used to be with old man Hodgson.'

Why would there be with Lane Forrester at the helm? grimaced Jenna tartly. As she knew from experience, he exuded a dynamic confidence that was difficult to resist, and when coupled with a far-sighted and astute intelligence, it made for an extremely successful combination in the business world.

Aloud, and despite having thought of their managing director as something of a dodderer herself on a number of occasions, she still felt bound to protest, 'That's not fair! After all, Mr Hodgson is pushing seventy. More than twice the age of the head of Forrester's.'

'Oh?' Kent's brows lifted in surprise. 'How do you know that? Has he been down to the plant too?'

Berating herself for having made such an unthinking remark, Jenna tried to rectify her mistake as nonchalantly as possible. 'No, I just happened to remember it from an article I read about him some time in one of the trade magazines.'

'I don't recall any such article,' Kent frowned. 'Which magazine would that have been, then?'

'I can't remember,' she prevaricated. 'And maybe it was in one that arrived while you were away on the road one time. Does it really matter?'

'Probably not,' he granted, to her relief. 'Although I suppose I should have guessed he was likely to be under forty too. Every other member of his staff that we've seen so far seems to have been.'

Jenna did an unconscious calculation. 'Actually, he's thirty-four,' she supplied, and then could have bitten her tongue out for having once again revealed a knowledge she would rather no one knew she possessed. It was evidently something she would have to watch very closely from now on.

Fortunately, Kent appeared to presume that was just another fact she had gleaned from the non-existent trade magazine, because his only comment was a slightly envious, 'Thirty-four, and already at the top of his field, eh? Half his luck!'

Luck had had nothing to do with it, as Jenna was aware, but this time made certain she did not commit another error by saying so, and merely responded with a seemingly concurring smile instead.

'Oh, well, at least there's one consolation in being a small cog in the corporate wheel,' he contended humorously, 'it provides one with a little leeway rather than having the big boss keeping an eagle eye on you all the time. In fact, it wouldn't surprise me if we never even get to see Forrester himself at all. Our little subsidiary will be too small a fish to warrant his personal attention, I'll be bound.'

'You really think so?' she questioned in hopeful tones. If that indeed turned out to be the case, no one would be more pleased than she would.

'I reckon,' he returned laconically before bidding her a final goodnight and starting down the stairs.

It was an assurance Jenna dwelt on happily as she made ready for bed, and which provided her with the first really untroubled sleep she had had since learning of the impending amalgamation. When she awoke the next morning the same feeling of having been reprieved was still with her, and as a result she set off for the office in her somewhat battered old Volkswagen in a more carefree frame of mind that she had done for some time.

On passing through the doors of the old brick administration building sited beside the small factory, though, she was greeted by an unexpected hive of activity and for a moment she stared about her in confusion. There seemed to be tradesmen everywhere! Already painters' trestles had been erected along one wall and dust sheets laid out to protect the furniture below. Not far from her own desk a couple of carpenters were well on their way to removing one of the heavy, wooden-grained windows that had so often broken her nails in her attempts to open them, while just inside the small reception area more workmen were beginning to relieve the floor of its old-fashioned, and in places, worn out linoleum covering.

'Isn't it terrific? The old place getting a face-lift at last,' enthused Holly, the young receptionist, as Jenna began moving past the front desk.

'Well, I won't say it didn't need it, but . . .'

'Our new boss certainly believes in instant action, doesn't he?' cut in Freda gaily as she joined them. 'Apparently he's a believer in pleasant surroundings making for better productivity. But you just wait until you meet him, you'll love him,' she continued with uncharacteristic fervour. 'He's a real charmer!'

'Is he ever!' added Holly, her eyes rolling expressively. 'I nearly fell off my chair when I found out why he was here. I never dreamt we'd be working for such an incredible hunk.'

Jenna suppressed an amused smile. She had known their new head office intended sending one of their own staff down to replace Mr Hodgson, but she gathered their managing director's replacement must be really something to have impressed Holly *and* Freda to such an extent.

'So just who is this macho personification of male attributes, then?' she quizzed drily.

Freda was only too willing to tell her: 'Unbelievably, it's none other than . . .'

'Lane Forrester himself!' Holly concluded excitedly for her.

'*Lane!*' The aghast exclamation burst forth from Jenna involuntarily, but on noting the strange looks it engendered on her companions' faces, tried to cover herself by passing it off with a shrug. 'It—it's an unusual name,' she smiled weakly. And so much for Kent's assumption! the dispiriting thought immediately followed. 'But why should he be concerning himself with such a relatively small concern? I would have thought he had more important matters requiring his attention.'

'Well, as I understand every subsidiary of the organisation is expected to pull its own weight, maybe he just likes the challenge of turning a rather unspectacular business into a successful one,' proposed Freda.

Or maybe he had just discovered his wife worked there and wanted the pleasure of firing her personally! Jenna speculated miserably, beginning to wish she had resigned when she had first considered it, and while she had still had the chance of escaping his notice.

'Anyway, since there's no one with him at the moment,' Freda went on cheerfully, 'I'll take you along and introduce you, then you'll be able to judge for yourself. He said he wanted to meet all the staff as soon as they arrived.'

Swallowing apprehensively, Jenna nodded her compliance. She supposed she had to come face to face with him sometime, so maybe the sooner she got it over and done with the better, but as she accompanied the older girl towards the building's largest office on distinctly shaky legs, her thoughts were nowhere near as resigned.

How on earth was she expected to acknowledge him? As a hitherto unknown employer, or as someone with whom she was already acquainted? But then, how could she do the latter when she had only just implied

he was a stranger to her? Besides, none of the staff
even knew she had been married, let alone to the very
man she was supposedly about to meet for the first
time! As well as that, and even more importantly
perhaps, what was he likely to say to her? Mockingly
greet her as his wife and them promptly inform her
that her services were no longer required? Or worse
still, if he was not already aware she worked there,
might not the shock make him refuse even to
acknowledge her at all? Oh, Lord, if only this meeting
had not been sprung on her with so little notice, she
groaned, sweeping her hair back from her face in a
distracted gesture as the appropriate office door
loomed large before them.

With her hand lifted to knock on the wooden
panelling, Freda gave a start when the door suddenly
swung open before her fingers could reach it, and a tall
male figure filled the opening.

'Oh, Mr Forrester, I was just . . .' Freda began with
a half laugh.

For Jenna's part, that was all she heard of the other
girl's introduction as she took an involuntary step
backwards, her wide spaced grey eyes connecting with
a pair of ebony lashed, hazel-green, and she felt a
warm flood of colour surge into her satin smooth
cheeks before it abruptly receded again as quickly as it
had arisen.

To her surprise, and considerable perturbation, her
initial thought was that he was still as damnably
attractive as he had ever been, but as that definitely
was not a feature she cared to be reminded of, she
determinedly forced the idea out of her mind and
concentrated on keeping her observations as dispassionate as possible. His dark brown hair was cut as

closely to his confidently held head as she remembered it, she noted; his eyes as alert and appraising; his firmly moulded mouth retaining the same slightly crooked curve above an inflexibly set jaw. The coffee coloured suit he was wearing was obviously custom tailored; the broad shouldered and lean hipped frame beneath just as obviously in peak condition; the unspoken force of his personality equally impossible to ignore.

Suddenly, on realising Freda had stopped speaking, Jenna sensed the other girl was waiting for her to say something now and, licking nervously at dry lips, she nodded stiffly and offered in a self-conscious murmur, 'Mr Forrester.'

'*Miss Bowman*,' he stressed significantly, although not too markedly, in return. Apart from an imperceptible tightening of his shapely mouth and the coolly assessing look that had entered his eyes when he first saw her, it was the only indication he had given that he even recognised her—much to Jenna's relief!

'Well, that was certainly brief and to the point,' remarked Freda in obvious surprise as Lane proceeded into Ian Leonard's new office. 'He's had quite a chat to everyone else so far.'

Something Jenna was unutterably grateful to have been spared! 'Yes, well, there probably isn't time for him to do that with all the office staff. I expect he's got a lot on his mind at the moment.'

'Mmm, I guess so,' Freda shrugged, allowing herself to be convinced. 'But what did you think of him? He's a whole heap better to look at than old Mr Hodgson, isn't he?'

'I'm surprised you should have noticed,' Jenna parried teasingly rather than answering directly. Lane was not a subject she wanted to discuss, in any shape or form. 'I thought you were a happily married woman and totally devoted to your husband.'

'Devoted, yes, but blind, no!' was the laughing retort. 'And Kent or no Kent, don't tell me you don't find him attractive too because I just wouldn't believe you!'

'All right then, I won't,' Jenna opted to neither confirm nor deny the contention. Then, in the hope of changing the topic altogether, 'So when was it decided that all this work should be done?' Indicating the busily employed tradesmen they had to skirt in order to reach their desks.

'Oh, some time last week, I believe,' Freda relayed offhandedly. 'You remember the feller who was wandering round the office for so long taking measurements, etcetera—I can't remember his name— well, apparently that's what he was here for.' Looking about her, she gave a light laugh. 'Not that I expected the transformation to begin quite this soon, though.'

Jenna replied with something appropriate but was thankful when the fair-haired girl finally continued on to her own desk. Although she supposed her first meeting with her husband after such a long time had not been as devastating as it could have been, or as she had anticipated, she still felt unbearably tense and apprehensive. Feelings that were in no way assuaged when Lane reappeared from her boss's office some minutes later and mockingly informed her that Ian wished to speak to her.

Automatically taking her notepad and pencil with her, Jenna entered the room hesitantly, unsure just what to expect. There had to have been *some* reason for that noticeably taunting note in Lane's voice. 'Mr

Forrester said you wanted to see me,' she murmured diffidently as she took her customary seat beside the window.

'Oh, yes . . . although not for dictation,' Ian smiled briefly on seeing the pad in her hand. His kindly features sobered again almost immediately. 'In fact, probably not for dictation ever again, unfortunately.'

Jenna could only stare at him mutely, her fingers clenching round her pencil so tightly she was amazed it didn't snap. So, she had been right in being wary of that goading tone of Lane's. She was going to be fired after all! Only he didn't have the guts to do it himself! she denounced bitterly.

'You see, Lane—Mr Forrester,' she suddenly realised Ian was continuing, 'has decided that since I'm new in this position now that Tom Morris has retired, it would be preferable if I took Freda as my secretary from now on seeing she knows where everything is that I might need as Tom's successor, and in turn you become his secretary.' Pausing, he sent her a rueful but resigned look. 'Although I'll be extremely sorry to lose you, of course, I must admit it does seem to be the best arrangement as what with all the changes that are about to take place, there'll undoubtedly be many instances when I'll need someone with a complete knowledge of how Tom ran things.'

From having been railing against the prospect of losing her job entirely, Jenna now found herself horrified at the thought of keeping it. 'You mean, I'll be working solely for . . . for Mr Forrester?' she gasped, only just managing to avoid calling him by his first name. 'But why me? Surely he must have a secretary of his own floating around somewhere!' A

resentful note began edging into her voice. No wonder
Lane had looked so mocking. He had known full well
that working in close proximity with him was the last
thing she would want!

Not surprisingly, Ian appeared somewhat nonplussed by the vehemence of her outburst. 'You're
saying, you don't want to work for him?' he sounded
in partly disbelieving accents.

She shrugged noncommittally, attempting to
camouflage her dismay. If she wasn't more careful she
would soon be arousing everyone's suspicions. 'I'd
rather continue working for you,' she answered
sincerely, hopefully.

'Yes, well, I'd be pleased if you could too, but
unfortunately . . .' He raised his shoulders in a helpless
gesture, and then gave a contrite laugh. 'Maybe I
shouldn't have given you such a glowing reference.
Though I don't think you'll find him a hard man to
work for. He seems a very decent type to me,' he
smiled encouragingly.

No doubt he was—to the rest of his employees!
mused Jenna whimsically. But not hard to work for
. . . well, that could be something else again. Where
she was concerned she did not expect it to be anything
but unadulterated purgatory! Not that she could say as
much to Ian, of course.

'Oh, well—them's the breaks, I guess,' she quipped
drily, emptily returning his smile only with an effort
as she rose to her feet. 'It would appear I've been
promoted.'

'That's probably the best way of looking at it,' Ian
endorsed, chuckling.

Back at her desk, Jenna had only just begun to
cursorily sort through her filing when the internal

phone rang, and with her thoughts still otherwise engaged she answered it absently.

'Where the hell have you been?' Lane's exasperated enquiry promptly cut in to her reverie.

Unconsciously, her head angled defiantly, even though he was not there to see it. 'Speaking with Ian Leonard . . . *as instructed!* she retorted.

'All this time? What did he do, make you a cup of tea in order to help you recover from the shock?'

'Since there was no shock—only a mild surprise— there was nothing to recover from,' she dulcetly contended, refusing to give him the pleasure of having her rise to his deliberate goading, or to admit just how alarmed she had been on learning of her new position. 'Ian merely took the trouble to explain why such a change was considered necessary, that's all.'

'Did he now?' The satirical inflection in his voice became noticeably pronounced. 'Well, as you obviously have no objections to the arrangement, perhaps you would care to bring your book in, together with the file on the new capacitor project, *Miss Bowman*.' Again that explicit emphasis which brought unbidden the ready colour to Jenna's cheeks. 'That is, *if* you can find it. The filing system in this place is a shambles!'

If he was referring to those cabinets in his office then she was inclined to agree with him. Unfortunately old Mr Hodgson had had a disconcerting habit of replacing papers in the first convenient space that happened to present itself. However, the opportunity was too good not to do a little return niggling of her own.

'If you're unable to find anything, *Mr* Forrester, you only have to ask and I'm sure it will prove no difficulty at all for one of us to immediately locate whatever you require,' she returned in lightly tart condescension.

'And if the files were in any reasonable order, I wouldn't need to waste my time asking, Miss Bowman!' There was more of a sting than a taunt in his tone now. 'So I might suggest you make it your first priority to ensure I can find what I want, when I want it!'

'Yes, *sir!*' she assented in exaggerated, but doubtful deference. 'As soon as possible, *sir!*'

'Jenna!' It was the first time he had used her christian name, and with such ominous softness that it had her involuntarily sucking in a nervous breath. 'Do you want to be thrown out on your ear?'

In view of what she was subjecting herself to in order to remain with the firm? 'N-not especially,' she owned jerkily, grudgingly.

'Then I recommend you forget the wisecracks and just get yourself in here . . . *now!*' he snapped, before slamming his phone down with a force that left her wincing.

A few minutes later, armed once more with her pad and pencil, Jenna knocked tentatively on her husband's door, and only entered the room when she heard his deep voice bidding her to do so. Having discarded his jacket and with his shirt sleeves rolled up to his elbows, Lane kept his hands resting on the desk as he leant back slightly, watching her approach with an impassive gaze.

'Do you always knock and then wait to be told to enter?' he surprised her by abruptly asking.

'Not usually, no,' she shrugged. 'Normally we just knock and then go straight in. Unless there's a visitor in the office, of course.'

'Then in order to save time I suggest you don't treat my office any differently,' he directed in ironic accents.

'I was only being polite.'

One dark brow rose smoothly, graphically upwards. 'It's a little late for that, isn't it?' Then, when she did not reply, his glance was centred significantly on the two articles she held in her hands. 'So where's the file I asked for? Or couldn't you find it either, after all?'

Determined once again not to allow him to nettle her, Jenna merely nodded towards the three filing cabinets standing against a side wall. 'It should be over there. Mr Hodgson was the last person to have it.'

'I've already looked through all of those!' she was informed on a testy note.

With her lips pressing together, Jenna headed for the cabinets without commenting, and being wise to their last managing director's foibles was able to locate the required folder before very long. Mainly because she was also aware of the other files Mr Hodgson had had out on his last day.

'Obviously not thoroughly enough, though, sir,' she did answer now, if somewhat tongue-in-cheek, as she laid the folder on his desk.

'Thank you.' Lane inclined his head briefly. 'But let's get one thing straight right from the start, shall we?' Suddenly he rose to his feet to tower menacingly over her. 'No one in my organisation calls me sir, least of all my own damned wife! Do I make myself clear?'

'As crystal!' she flared sarcastically. 'But you needn't think I'm going to call you *Mr* Forrester either!'

'I wouldn't expect you to! The name's obviously too

distasteful for you, isn't it, *Miss Bowman?*' he ground
out savagely.

'I thought you'd prefer not to have a *Mrs* Forrester
on the scene,' she threw back at him, flippantly
protective.

A muscle stirred at the side of Lane's uncompromising jaw. 'Except that the sun hasn't yet risen on the
day when you'd put consideration for someone else
before your own wishes!'

'Oh, and you always did, I suppose!' Her grey eyes
widened facetiously. 'I mean, you used to come home
before midnight so infrequently that I'm surprised
you even realised you had a wife!'

'And you knew damned well why I was working
such long hours! Because I had to repair the damage
done by leaving too much control of the business in
other people's hands while I was trying to satisfy your
capricious whims!' he rasped. 'Besides, what would
have been the point of me coming home earlier? You
were rarely there anyway! You were too busy enjoying
the social whirl . . . remember?'

'Only because I had to have *some* company, and I
had to fill in my time somehow!' Jenna flashed
defensively.

'Even after the baby was born?'

Jenna turned deathly pale, her anger rapidly
evaporating and leaving only anguish in its stead as
Lane's bleak words stabbed at her relentlessly. Oh,
God, why had he had to bring that up? she despaired
brokenly. It had taken her years to finally come to
terms, outwardly at least, with the tragedy of their tiny
daughter's death, but the knowledge that if she had
not gone out that particular evening the unnecessary
accident would probably never have occurred, had still

left scars on her conscience that she knew would never fade.

It had all happened so innocently, so unexpectedly, she recalled with a convulsive shudder. Because she had been going to a party that night—without Lane, as usual—she had arranged for their usual teen-aged baby sitter to look after twelve months old Kerryn, just as she had on numerous other such occasions.

Only that particular evening young Dena, usually so reliable, had been bathing the baby when her boyfriend called at the house and, intending to leave Kerryn happily playing with her toys in the bath for only a moment, she had gone to answer the door. Admittedly, she had not invited the boy inside, but at the same time she had apparently stayed talking to him for longer than she realised, because when she finally returned to the bathroom it was to discover the baby face down in the water and no amount of resuscitation able to revive the still little form.

The poor little girl had been distraught when she phoned Jenna with the mind-numbing news, and the event had set the final seal on Jenna and Lane's marriage. He had blamed her for leaving the child with a baby sitter—as indeed she blamed herself—but in defence she would not admit any such thing and simply countered with the accusation that if he had been planning to arrive home at a decent hour then she would not have gone out in the first place.

After that things had merely gone from bad to worse. When she had shown few visible signs of grief (because they had been too tightly bottled up inside her at that stage), Lane had maintained it was due to relief at being rid of the child because then she did not have to spare any of her time on anything but the pursuit of her own pleasure. While, in retaliation, because the day after the depressing funeral he was back to being as engrossed in his work as he had ever been, she had charged that as the baby had only been a girl, and not the boy he would undoubtedly have preferred, it had not appeared to cause him much sorrow anyway.

In the weeks that followed Jenna could remember needing Lane's company more than ever but neither her pride, nor her feelings of guilt, would allow her to ask for it, let alone acknowledge it on those few occasions when he did spend some time at home. Eventually, after about three months of such tortured misery, she had known she had to leave the increasingly strained atmosphere altogether if she was ever to recover from the agonising experience, and with just a terse note to Lane advising him she would not be returning, she had gone back to the soothing surroundings of her parents' home.

Now all those carefully repressed memories had been callously wrenched back to the forefront of her mind again and, unmindful of the tears spilling on to her thick lashes, Jenna gazed up at her husband contemptuously.

'You pitiless bastard! I wish to God I'd never set eyes on you again!' she breathed in low, choking tones. 'You just couldn't wait to bring that up again, could you? Just as you'd never let me forget it before! It always did give you a sense of satisfaction to hold—to hold Kerryn's death over my head, didn't it, Lane?'

'Did it?' he countered on a bitter, rough-edged note, his eyes narrowing coldly. 'How would you know? You were always too absorbed in your own self-pity to even care, much less be aware, how I felt about *anything!*' Halting, he raked a hand through his hair savagely and expelled a heavy breath. 'In any event, as it so happens, and whether you choose to believe it or not, I didn't intend to mention the baby in any context. It simply slipped out in the heat of the moment, that's all.' With a sigh, he shook his head wearily. 'However, as none of this has anything to do with why we're here, I might suggest we make an effort to keep the past and the present separate, and just get on with the dictation I originally called you in to take.'

Dictation! He thought she could calmly take notes after just having been heartlessly reminded of the most devastating period of her life! What did he think she was? As insensitive and unfeeling as himself? Jenna condemned scathingly, and in a moment of stormy resentment flung her pad and pencil across the room.

'To hell with your damned dictation!' she cried. 'And if that means I'm fired, I don't care! Do you hear me? I don't care!' She began to sob helplessly as she turned for the door.

'Jenna ... for God's sake!' Two forceful hands suddenly gripped her shaking shoulders and spun her close to a broad chest. 'You can't go out into the office in that state.'

'I don't care!' she repeated, shaking her head wildly and whipping long strands of silky hair about her damp cheeks as she fought vainly to free herself.

Restraining her easily with one hand, Lane brushed the hair back from her face with his other in a surprisingly gentle movement. 'So you keep insisting, although I doubt it's entirely true,' he declared somewhat wryly.

'Why? Because it's unheard of for any female not to

want to work for the ultramasculine Lane Forrester?'
she attempted a tearful gibe. She could still remember
the effect her virile husband had always had on other
members of her own sex.

'No, because if you hadn't wanted to remain you
would have resigned immediately you discovered just
which company was buying this one out!'

'I c-considered it, b-believe me!' Her voice shook
uncontrollably. 'B-but how was I to know you'd take a
p-personal interest in the firm?'

'You should have,' he returned sardonically. 'I
always do in new ventures . . . as I also did during our
time together.'

She had not realised. Not that it mattered now,
anyway. 'Well, whether I c-care or not is immaterial
really, isn't it?' she claimed on a rising note, her eyes
blurring involuntarily once more. 'So why don't you
just get on with it and fire me? Or does it give you a
twisted sense of power to keep me in suspense?' She
struck out at him blindly.

'Anything but, you overwrought little virago!' Lane
repudiated fiercely, succinctly, and with no gentleness
at all in either of his hands now as he gave her a
violent shake.

Jenna's attempts to escape became increasingly
turbulent. 'Because you've something even more
vengeful in mind?' she jeered in retaliation.

'Don't tempt me!' he bit out corrosively, and
hauling her towards the chair in front of his desk,
thrust her into it without ceremony. With his hands
resting on the wooden arms on either side of her, he
leant forward overpoweringly. 'But mainly because I
have a mound of work to get through, and for that I
need a secretary!'

Momentarily, the only sound in the room was that of their quickened breathing as she stared at him confusedly. 'You mean . . .' her eyes strayed compulsively to where her notebook and pencil lay scattered on the floor, 'you're not dismissing me?'

The line of his shapely mouth took on a caustic curve. 'The message finally got through, did it?'

Jenna's thoughts were too chaotic for her to take exception to the sarcasm. In fact, she was unsure as to whether she was even relieved at having retained her job. 'But—but why?' she faltered. 'You could have used one of the other girls in the office.'

'Except they don't happen to be acquainted with the various projects either in operation, or under consideration. You do!' he stressed with a brief nod. 'So I'm sorry, my love,' in a distinctly mocking, certainly not affectionate tone, 'but it would appear that whether we like it or not, for the time being at least we're stuck with each other.' It was his eyes that glanced meaningfully at her discarded tools of trade this time. 'Even if it does seem likely you're going to be the most volatile secretary I've ever had.'

His action only served to remind Jenna of the reason for them being there and she had to press her lips together to stop their trembling. 'It's no use, Lane,' she began unsteadily. 'If we needed any proof, this morning has just shown how impossible it would be for us to work together. One word about—about . . .' leaving the name unsaid, she hurried on, 'and we would only be at each other's throats all over again.'

'You think I don't know that?' His voice was harsh as he swung away to stand rubbing at the back of his neck with an impatient hand.

Her shimmering grey eyes shaded with uncertainty.

'W-well, then?' Lane drew in a deep breath and turned back to face Jenna dispassionately. 'Then we'll just have to ensure she isn't mentioned, won't we?'

Jenna chewed at her lip in silent contemplation. 'I suppose so,' she finally had little option but to agree, albeit a trifle doubtfully. Under the circumstances it seemed the only logical solution, but whether it would also prove to be a practical one, only time would tell.

CHAPTER TWO

THE following couple of weeks were something of an eye-opener for Jenna, as she came to realise just how much of the necessary effort required to have Forrester's newest subsidiary heading upwards financially once again, would be expended by her husband. Of course she had always known he possessed an instinctive flair for business, and for recognising those products most likely to capture the public's fancy; but it was not until he began reviewing the various new manufacturing projects the company had planned, that she actually learnt just how competent and imaginative a design engineer he was as well.

He also worked at an unrelenting pace, she soon discovered ruefully, but as this seemed to preclude many opportunities for comments of a personal nature she was inclined to feel the benefits outweighed the disadvantages; even though it meant her working hours were extended more often than not—and quite drastically so on occasion. An occurrence Kent found nowhere near as acceptable, however, because on those few evenings when Jenna was able to share his company she was usually too drained to want to do anything but sleep.

'For heaven's sake, you're not working late again tonight, are you?' he made his increasingly common complaint yet again one afternoon on hearing Jenna apologise for not being available to go to the movies with him that evening. 'This is getting past the point of a joke, you know! The man's becoming a positive slave-driver,' he said with a disgruntled look in the direction of Lane's office, 'and I'm sure all this working back can't really be necessary.'

'Lane apparently thinks it is,' she shrugged, smiling contritely.

A reply that did not appear to mollify him for his eyes promptly narrowed suspiciously. 'And that's another thing! I notice it didn't take you long to get on first name terms with him,' he growled.

'Well, so is practically everyone else,' she half laughed in surprise.

'The bosses, maybe, but not the rest of us . . . and certainly not the office staff!' his retort came explicitly.

Until then Jenna had not really paid the matter any attention—probably because she had been too busy to take note of anything much at all besides her work of late; but now that it had been pointed out to her she suddenly realised it was the truth, and that not even Freda called their new boss anything but Mr Forrester.

'I—well—it just came about through our working so closely together, I guess,' she offered hastily. After their disturbing confrontation on the subject it had appeared the only sensible course to adopt.

'But working so closely . . . at what, I'm beginning to wonder!'

'Kent!' She gazed up at him, shocked. Not only was his insinuation the last thing she had expected, as well as being the least likely to occur, but it was also the last thing she wanted anyone to suspect. It might give rise to the further speculation that she and Lane were not perhaps the strangers everyone to date had assumed them to be! 'You're letting your imagination run away with you,' she chided with forced humour. 'Why on earth would Lane—or Mr Forrester, if you prefer,' she amended diplomatically, 'be interested in me? To him, I'm just another secretary with a requisite knowledge of shorthand and a set of nimble fingers, that's all.' And just to be on the safe side, in case he still had any doubts, it did not seem unreasonable to divulge, 'Besides, from what I've heard, he's already married, anyway.'

Kent evidently did not see it in the same light. 'So when did that ever stop a man in his position from wanting the best of both worlds?' he immediately sneered.

Strangely, considering his fatal attraction for the opposite sex, that was one transgression she had not accused her husband of during their years together, Jenna recollected absently, then shook her head quickly to dismiss the past.

'When *I* happen to be the secretary involved, that's when!' she now answered in tautly indignant tones. 'And if those are the only type of remarks you intend to make, then I'm afraid you'll have to excuse me, because I'm rather busy at the moment.' She lowered her head and began flicking over the pages of her notebook.

For a minute or two Kent stood looking down at her indecisively, and then he gave a remorseful sigh. 'Oh, hell, I'm sorry,' he apologised. 'Actually, that wasn't what I meant to say at all. Forgive me . . .?' He bent to look into her face with cajoling eyes.

'Only if you stop making such ridiculous innuendoes.' She aggrievedly returned his gaze.

'I will, I promise,' he vowed, and lifting a hand

touched it lightly to her cheek. 'It's just that you're so damned beautiful I can't picture any other man being immune to you either.'

Jenna flushed and looked about her anxiously, hoping no one else had overheard, and as if sensing her self-consciousness at his choice of place for such words, Kent continued hurriedly.

'As a matter of fact, what I was really going to say, or ask you, was if you'd like to spend next weekend at my parents' place up at Woy Woy. We could do a spot of sailing, drop in a line for some fishing, or just go to the beach. I thought it would make a nice change as well as give you the chance to relax a bit after all this extra work you've been doing of late. Quite apart from allowing us to have a little more time together,' he added engagingly.

'Sounds great, and just what I need.' It didn't take her long to agree. She had visited his parents twice before and she liked both of them, and the small coastal resort where they lived about an hour or so's drive north of the city. 'When did you plan to leave? Friday night, as usual?'

'Mmm, I thought straight after work, and then we'll be there in time for dinner,' he said, looking considerably happier now. 'Providing, of course, you won't be working late that night as well!' His mouth shaped wryly.

Jenna laughed, her smoky grey eyes sparkling brightly. 'Yes, well, I'll just have to do my best to ensure . . .'

'If it's not too much trouble, *Miss Bowman*, might I ask just when I'm going to receive that blueprint I asked you to get for me over half an hour ago?' The abrasively emphasised request suddenly cut across

Jenna's words and had her jumping a trifle guiltily as she swung to face her husband's office and found him to be standing in the doorway with his hands resting on lean hips and a decidedly less than pleased expression on his tightly set features.

'Oh—er—the plant said they'd send it right across,' she stammered awkwardly, wondering just how long he had been there and if he had heard any of their conversation.

Lane's brows lifted sarcastically. 'I still don't have it, though.'

'I—I'll go and see what's happened to it,' she offered swiftly, already rising to her feet. Anything to escape the penetrating gaze that was surveying both herself, and the man beside her, with such assessing shrewdness.

'Thank you,' he acknowledged, sardonically mocking; but to her relief, then returned inside his office without another word.

'Oh, brother!' Kent released an expressive breath. 'He can make you feel like a kid caught with your hand in the cookie jar just by looking at you, can't he?' Pausing, he frowned curiously. 'But what was with the heavily stressed Miss Bowman bit? He doesn't normally call you that, does he? I mean, not while you're using his first name, surely!'

'Oh, no, that's just his way of getting his point across,' Jenna dismissed the question casually. And she knew exactly which point too! with an annoyed, inward grimace. If he did it too often he would be raising queries that could not be shrugged off quite so nonchalantly. 'He knows I've got a lot to do and he probably didn't like the idea of my stopping in order to talk to you.'

'It was only for a couple of minutes!'

A quick look at the wall clock and she modified wryly, 'Twenty, at least.'

'In that case, I guess I had better make myself scarce,' he half laughed. 'I've got an appointment with one of our customers in town shortly, anyway, so I'll see you tomorrow, okay?'

Jenna smiled and nodded, her steps already putting distance between them. After all, she *was* busy at the moment, and since the time had sped past so quickly during their conversation, the added walk across to the manufacturing plant and back was not going to do anything at all to help her to catch up.

Luckily she met the apprentice bringing the blueprint across just before she reached the factory, so she at least did not have to wait around while they searched for it—the reason for it not having been delivered sooner, apparently—and with it safely in her keeping she returned to the office as rapidly as possible.

Knocking only perfunctorily on Lane's door, she entered the room immediately, and then came to a stunned and mortified halt on finding he not only had a female visitor with him, but that he was in the process of kissing her extremely thoroughly.

For a second Jenna just stood there, transfixed, her cheeks staining with a rush of embarrassed colour, her thoughts a jumble. Unaccountably, she abruptly realised there was more than a little resentment mixed in with her humiliation at discovering another woman held so securely within her husband's arms. Which, of course, was absolutely idiotic! she promptly railed at herself irately. Why should she care how many women he was playing around with? It was nothing to her, she had Kent to interest her now, and whatever Lane did did not affect her in the slightest.

Nonetheless, as a result of having entered with so little ceremony, it soon became obvious it was too late to back out quietly again as the couple in front of her parted—although without any haste, and certainly not with any sign of the self-consciousness she was experiencing, she observed somewhat acidly—and two pairs of eyes focused on her coolly.

'I—I'm sorry ... I didn't realise ... I w-wasn't aware you had a visitor,' she faltered without quite looking at either of them, but turning slightly more towards Lane. She had never seen the woman before, in any event. Had no idea as to who she might be, in fact, although it was apparent from the superbly simple lines of her faultlessly cut silk dress that thrift was not a consideration she ever had to practise. Indeed, wealth was stamped all over her from the top of her salon styled ash blonde hair, to the soles of her softest kid shoes. 'I—umm—just wanted to give you this as soon as possible.' She waved the blueprint in front of her distractedly. 'But if you're otherwise engaged, I'll ...' Swallowing convulsively and with her face flaming anew, she came to a stop, suddenly realising the construction that could be placed upon her words. Now she did take a step backwards. A hasty, though still obviously indecisive step.

'Oh, for crying out loud!' Lane's roughly exasperated voice reached out to her. 'Just put the plan on the desk, will you, Jenna, and stop looking as if you've just stumbled on to something wickedly licentious! Or don't you and your boyfriend believe in indulging in such immoral behaviour as kissing?' he mocked, and his girl-friend tittered in undisguised amusement.

At that Jenna did look up, her gaze beginning to smoulder as it connected with his taunting one, and she moved closer. So he knew, or had guessed, Kent was not merely an office acquaintance, had he? Well, that still did not give him the right to set her up as a figure of fun in front of his haughty-faced friend!

'Why, of course we believe in sex, Mr Forrester,' she made herself smile sweetly, deliberately being more explicit, and just as purposely using the name she knew would irritate him as she pushed rather than put the folded paper she was holding into his hand. 'It's just that we prefer a little more privacy for our amorous activities, that's all.'

The goading light in his eyes was replaced by a chilling one. 'As we had, before you burst in uninvited!'

She hunched a shoulder in simulated deprecation. 'I said I was sorry, and it was *your* idea for me not to wait before entering,' she reminded on a whimsical note.

'Unless I had visitors!'

'Yes, well, if I hadn't had to leave my desk in order to get that drawing for you,' which would now undoubtedly remain untouched until his companion departed! 'I would have known, wouldn't I? But as it was . . .' She spread her hands expressively, artlessly wide.

'Oh, does it really matter, darling?' put in the blonde in bored accents from where she had seated, or rather, draped herself languidly in a leather studded armchair. 'I have no objections to anyone knowing how I feel about you. Although I am just dying for something to drink and a cigarette, despite finding I haven't any of my special brand with me.' Her baby blue eyes turned in Jenna's direction. 'Go and get me some, there's a good girl. I've written it all down so you can't make a mistake.' Tearing off the lower half of a page of Lane's calendar she held it out limply, as if even that much effort should not have been required of her.

Jenna accepted it from her mechanically, although her thoughts were not anywhere near as accommodating. She was already bristling in unpredictable outrage again in response to that possessive endearment and the woman's nonchalantly expressed emotions, and now anger was added to her feelings of affront. How dared she treat her as if she was some errand girl with nothing better to do than run her messages!

'I'll see if one of the juniors has time to get them for you,' she said stiffly. If they were an unusual brand, as had sounded likely, it was evident neither of their two closest corner stores would be likely to stock them.

'Oh, no, not a junior!' The suggestion was immediately discounted in unbearably patronising tones. 'They would be bound to bring back the wrong thing, as I've had happen before. No, you go yourself. Flora always does, doesn't she, Lane?'

'Certainly,' he concurred smoothly, his mouth sloping lazily as stormy grey eyes were raised to his. 'My permanent secretary is always most helpful.'

Well, good for her! flared Jenna mutinously, her resentment escalating rapidly on deducing he apparently did not intend to inform his girl-friend that his staff were not there solely to cater to her every wish.

'I thought you wanted that report typed as quickly as possible,' she ground out in a seething mutter.

He flexed his broad shoulders negligently, his expression mocking. 'That didn't appear to worry you while you were talking to Sharman, and as I'm sure you'll agree that Miss Cornell's company is rather more important than a mere sales rep, then I've no doubt that finding a little more time to fulfil her small request should equally present no problem for you.'

Except that, in consequence, she would be working even later that evening than she had at first envisaged—as he damned well knew! But—so that was who the blonde was, Rosalind Cornell, was it? Jenna's perusal of the trade magazines legitimately came in handy this time. Apparently her father, the founder of a large chain of electrical retail outlets, had died only a few months before, leaving his only daughter in charge of the commercial empire he had built. No wonder she was able to dress like a million dollars! However, since it seemed she was not to be given any choice but to personally chase off on the woman's errand, she was not about to do so in a particularly helpful manner.

'And just where do I get the money for these cigarettes?' There was no way she was going to use her own, and Rosalind Cornell certainly had not offered any.

'From petty cash, naturally!' Lane retorted in caustic overtones. 'Where did you think?'

Her features assumed an injured cast. 'You could have wanted it as a private transaction,' she mumured, looking down at the piece of paper in her hand. 'But how much should I take? I've no idea what they're likely to cost.' She had not even recognised the brand, let alone could guess at their price.

Lane drew an aggravated breath, and with an excusing smile for his visitor, caught hold of Jenna's upper arm in a steely grip to start hustling her towards the door. 'Try using your own discretion, you

obstructive little so-and-so!' he instructed pungently.
'But I'm warning you, Jenna! Don't think you can
play smart by saying you couldn't find any, or by
returning with the wrong ones, because I can assure
you it isn't going to work. You'll just be sent back
again until you do find them!'

'I'm a secretary . . . not a messenger!' she glared at
him indignantly.

'While you're in my employ you'll fill any position I
designate!'

'Particularly if that means I can be made to run
around after all your girl-friends, I suppose?' she
surmised on a low, furious note.

'I must admit it does have a certain—how shall I
put it?' one dark brow rose to a taunting peak,
'retaliatory appeal?' He uttered a short, mirthless
laugh. 'Although I fail to see just what grounds you
have for complaint when it was your choice that we
part company five years ago.'

Jenna bit at her lip sharply, apprehensive that he
may have been intending to drag up more of the past.
'No, I guess not,' she acquiesced suddenly, and
evidently to his surprise as his ensuing look of partly
frowned speculation showed, but simultaneously
determining to deprive him of at least some of that
retaliatory appeal by refusing to display, outwardly
anyway, any further resentment concerning Rosalind
Cornell's request. Besides, the beginnings of an idea
were forming as to how she could avoid this particular
one being repeated, and with her expression studiously
bland, she shrugged resignedly. 'So I'll get the money
from Terry, shall I?'

'Since he's in charge of the petty cash, it would
seem reasonable.' There was still a touch of

contemplation amidst the emerging irony it afforded her some pleasure to note. For once, he was the one just a little unsure of his ground.

'And will you sign for it, or will it be all right if I do?'

'Oh, I hardly think some cigarettes are likely to exceed your limit, so why don't you sign . . . and then maybe you'll stop asking such damned superfluous questions!'

'Sorry.' She hunched one shoulder diffidently. 'I simply wanted to make sure, that's all.' Make sure things went her way, she qualified to herself.

'The only thing you need make certain of, is that you return with what you were requested to purchase,' declared Lane as a last chafing parting shot before returning his attention to his visitor.

As Jenna had deduced, Rosalind Cornell's particular brand of cigarettes were impossible to obtain anywhere with a reasonable radius of the factory, and as time progressed and she was forced to travel further and further afield, the fuse on her temper became shorter and shorter. It was a very hot day and having to keep climbing in and out of a boiling car, as well as having to walk quite some distance on occasion when nearby parking spaces were not available, did absolutely nothing to help cool her rising temperature.

In fact, by the time she did actually locate a shop that sold the required brand, she was hot, tired and simmering! Even the thought of having successfully carried out her plan was not enough to sustain her now, and the knowledge that she still had all her work to do only provided more fuel for an ever mounting fire. When she finally made it back to the office again it was almost time for the rest of the staff to finish for the day, which was not an exactly soothing thought either, and she strode between the intervening desks with her eyes fixed balefully on the wood panelled door at the end of the room.

Pounding, rather than knocking on the door, she perhaps should not have been surprised when Lane opened it himself instead of merely advising her to enter, but she was, and it took her a moment to recover—her breath mainly! When she did, it was to thrust the thin plastic carrier-bag containing the cigarettes into his hand furiously.

'As requested!' she snapped fierily, and about-facing, promptly began pacing for her desk.

'Jenna!' Her name was bitten out wrathfully, piercingly, behind her.

Halting, she took a deep, though not very steadying breath, and spun around again, her head held challengingly high. 'Yes?'

'In here, thank you!' Lane indicated his office with a curt nod.

With her breasts heaving, she continued to eye him defiantly. 'I've got a lot of typing to do . . . as you may recall!' she gibed.

'*In here*, I said!' he grated thunderously.

Briefly, Jenna seriously considered refusing—why should she have to endure another session of his goading comments in front of his patronising girlfriend?—but on noticing they were also starting to receive some interested glances from the other members of the staff, she finally yielded and flounced past him into, of all things, an empty office. A discovery that was the last straw as far as she was concerned and had her rounding on him infuriatedly as soon as the door was closed.

'Are you telling me, that after all the trouble I had to go to in order to get those damned things,' gesturing violently towards the parcel he was now placing on the desk, 'that she couldn't even be bothered,' or have the decency! 'to wait until I returned with them?' she demanded.

'No, I'm afraid you were gone so long that Miss Cornell couldn't stay any longer,' she was informed on a wry note. Now that the rest of the staff were unable to see or hear, it appeared he regarded the situation as, if not amusing, then at least definitely less of a threat to his authority.

Not unexpectedly, it was not a change Jenna either missed, or appreciated. 'That's because I had to drive all the way back to Burwood just to find a shop that sold them!' she blazed irately.

Lowering himself into his chair, Lane surveyed her furious features long and hard, and then his lips tilted crookedly. 'Why don't you just sit down, Jenna.' It was a recommendation not a request, but which was totally ignored. 'If I might say so, you look flushed and somewhat dishevelled.'

'I wonder why?' Her wide-spaced eyes rounded facetiously. 'After all, it's only about thirty-seven degrees outside, and at least ten degrees hotter than that in the car!'

'Your car?'

'No, the Prime Minister's!' she quipped, heavily sarcastic.

Momentarily his lips thinned. 'Then maybe you would have done better to have taken one of the company's air-conditioned vehicles!'

'Except that yours is the only authority on which I could have done that, but at the time you apparently had other things besides work on your mind to even think of mentioning it!' she retorted mockingly, resentfully.

Lane leant forward, his sable framed gaze holding hers inexorably, his demeanour altering indefinably. 'Sit down, Jenna!' he ordered rather than suggested this time, and sensing the subtle change in his mood she finally complied, grudgingly. Having already vented most of her annoyance she was starting to feel a little calmer now, anyway. 'I'd like to get one thing clear,' he went on, resting his chin on the back of a closed and upraised hand and continuing to eye her intently. 'Just who are you supposed to be addressing with all these incensed remarks, my pet? Your employer . . . or your husband?'

'I don't have a husband!' she swiftly denied in vehement tones. Although she was honest enough to admit, to herself at least, that having him as her boss definitely had more than a little to do with it. She had certainly never spoken to any other employer in such a manner. Would never have thought of doing so, if the truth were known. Then again, if it came to that, she had never before worked for anyone who would, or could, goad her to such an extent either! 'If I did have, I hardly expect he'd be sending me on errands for his mistress!' The charge was thrown at him hotly.

'Only Rosalind doesn't happen to be my mistress, whereas even if you would evidently rather it were otherwise, you *do* still happen to be my wife!' he returned with just the hint of a rasp in his voice. 'And the reason you were sent out for some of her cigarettes was purely in the cause of business. She happens to be a valued client.'

'Mmm, I could tell by the businesslike way you

were kissing her when I walked in!' she burst out acrimoniously before she could stop it. Why should it matter to her who he kissed, or in what manner?

Lane merely slanted her a taunting smile. 'Oh, I didn't say we only had a business relationship. Just that she wasn't my mistress—which implies a certain permanency,' he drawled.

Meaning, he preferred to play the field instead of being confined to just one! Jenna supposed with a grimace, and feeling oddly dispirited. She was also beginning to suspect why he had never applied for a divorce. Something that had continually surprised her until now. It was becoming obvious that being married, but separated, afforded him a convenient protection, while at the same time permitting him to behave as if he were completely unattached.

'However, to return to my original question,' Lane interrupted her moody thoughts in a cooling manner. 'Then if, as would seem to be the case, your apparently offended declarations are all for your employer, I might advocate that you voice them a little more circumspectly, because I've never accepted insolent backchat from any other secretary I may have had in the past, and I certainly don't intend to start now! Understand?'

Jenna's lips pulled into a disgruntled downward curve. 'Oh, unhesitatingly, s——' She broke off abruptly, flinching, when a hand suddenly shot across the desk to wrap around her wrist in a bruising grip.

'Don't say it, Jenna, or you could find the consequences even less pleasant than you do now!' he threatened harshly. 'I told you before what I thought of that "sir" caper of yours!'

'So you did,' she acceded with some asperity,

refusing to show any further sign after that first
instinctive recoil as to how much his grasp hurt. The
bones in her wrist felt close to snapping and she could
not help but wonder if he realised the pressure he was
exerting, then decided he probably knew but did not
care. 'Although I notice you aren't so particular about
not calling me Miss Bowman in that emphasising
fashion all the time! You'll have not only Kent, but
everyone else suspicious as well soon, if you keep it up!'

'You chose to revert to your maiden name,' he
shrugged unconcernedly. 'Besides, why should
Sharman . . .' He paused, his eyes half closing astutely,
a sardonic smile beginning to catch at his firmly
defined mouth. 'You mean, he doesn't know you've
ever been married?'

'Yes, he knows, although no one else in the office
does, but—but he thinks I—I'm divorced,' she
divulged reluctantly, berating herself for having
mentioned Kent in the first place.

Lane's smile turned into an even more satirical
laugh, but he did at least release his hold on Jenna's
wrist, for which she was thankful. Her skin smarted
painfully and only by massaging it could she relieve
some of the soreness.

'He is in for a surprise then, isn't he?' he stated in
obvious amusement.

'What do you mean?' Jenna stopped rubbing at her
wrist as she gazed at him warily. He could not intend
telling Kent, could he?

'If he should propose.'

'He already has.' Relief had her speaking without
thinking again, and immediately biting at her lip in
dismay. She had not meant to reveal anything of the
kind. Certainly no one else knew as much.

'Oh?' A noticeable amount of his previous humour disappeared. 'To which your reply was . . .?'

Jenna inhaled deeply. 'That's none of your business, Lane!' she defied. 'In fact, nothing I do these days is any concern of yours!' she added just to ensure he fully understood her feelings on the matter. 'And as I do still have all my work to finish because of this afternoon's little jaunt, I think it's time I got on with it . . . if that's all you want to say, of course.' She started to rise.

Lane flexed one shoulder indifferently, although there was nothing at all dispassionate about his predominantly green gaze. It followed her with a speculative persistence she found somewhat unnerving.

'You've forgotten something, haven't you?' He did not speak until she had almost reached the door, and then only in such a bland voice that she had no idea just what thoughts may have been running through his mind.

'I don't think so.' She shook her head slightly as she half turned back again.

He waved a hand towards the carrier-bag still lying where he had left it. 'This can't all be cigarettes, it's too large. There has to be something of yours here as well.'

'No.' Jenna shook her head again, and had to press her lips together in an effort to control their irrepressible urge to smile. 'Miss Cornell did ask for *some* cigarettes, as I remember.'

With twin furrows of suspicion making an appearance between his brows, Lane summarily dragged the bag closer and looked inside. 'You bought four *cartons*!' His voice rang with condemnation.

'I wasn't to know how many *some* constituted in Miss Cornell's estimation,' she excused in falsely defensive accents. 'She could be an extremely heavy smoker for all I'm aware. I just tried to do the right thing by her, as I believed you wanted me to. Her being such an obviously—umm—cherished client, and all.' Now she did smile. A scornfully provoking widening of her mobile mouth that, to her amazement, had him regarding her wryly.

'While conveniently precluding any further such errands on your own behalf, hmm?'

'Gee, I never thought of that.' Her thickly lashed eyes brimmed with innocence.

'No, I bet you didn't!' That contemplative look that had so unsettled her previously, made a sudden reappearance. 'But for your information, I said Rosalind was a valued client . . . not a cherished one,' he corrected drily.

'Oh, dear, poor woman, and her just doting on you too,' she dared to mock.

Lane's expression tightened. 'You're pushing your luck, Jenna! So why don't you just leave, before you really succeed in riling me.'

Shrugging, Jenna did as advised, gauging it a prudent time to depart—for once she felt as if not quite everything had gone her husband's way—but still unable to resist quipping in a stage whisper as she opened the door, 'First you're ordered in, then you're ordered out. I wish . . .'

'*Jenna!*' A rasping growl assailed her ear, cutting her off in mid-sentence.

'All right! I'm going, I'm going,' she assured him, dubiously straight-faced, and closed the door between them while the darkly menacing look on his face was still only that, a look, and nothing more shattering.

Unfortunately for Jenna her sense of victory was only a passing one because Lane remained in the same short-tempered mood for the rest of the evening. Even during their dinner break his attitude showed no signs of changing so that she was relieved to get back to work immediately it was over. A feeling that was to alter radically as soon as he began finding fault whenever and wherever possible—and whether justified or not! she fumed on many instances—and making modifications with a kind of caustic pleasure that shortly had her emotions running almost as high as they had been when she returned to the office late that afternoon by the time her work was eventually completed.

Clipping the required enclosures to her last letter she took it in to him to sign and waited tautly while he read it. She was half expecting him to discover something wrong with this one too, just for the hell of it, although she knew there was not a mistake in it. On this occasion, however, Lane merely put his signature to it cursorily before handing it back to her and she sighed thankfully.

'Since that's the last, I'll be leaving now, if there's nothing else you want me to do,' she said stiltedly.

Lane acknowledged the remark with a short nod, which Jenna took for acceptance and promptly headed for the door, anxious to make good her exit before he perhaps changed his mind.

'Oh, by the way . . .' She had only taken a few steps before his voice had her swinging back again, apprehensively, the very casualness of his tone making her instantly wary. 'I shall be needing your services this weekend for a conference I'm having at home, so don't make any plans, will you?' he directed coolly.

With her worst fears realised, Jenna glared at him furiously. 'I already have!' she shot back.

His brows peaked in a gesture of supreme indifference. 'Then you'll just have to cancel them, won't you?'

'No, I will not!' she refused hotly. 'Why should I? I work practically all hours now, and I'm entitled to a break over the weekend at least!'

'Naturally,' he conceded, but so smoothly that she did not suppose for one moment that he intended to relent. 'Except on this occasion when matters of some importance will be discussed and the ensuing report requires typing.'

'So why can't your permanent secretary do it? Why does it have to be me?'

'Because the matters we'll mainly be dealing with concern this particular subsidiary, and that, my pet,' with taunting overtones, 'makes you the most logical selection.'

'Jenna's breasts rose and fell rapidly. 'But not *this* weekend!' she heaved. 'It's unfair to expect me to change my arrangements on such short notice, and especially since I've made plans for going away.'

'With Sharman?'

The silkiness with which the query was delivered immediately had her gazing at him askance. Could he possibly have heard her and Kent making their arrangements, and then deliberately decided on this conference simply as a means to thwart her plans? She would not put it past him, and it would certainly explain why she had not heard it mentioned previously! The thought had her eyes holding his defiantly.

'Yes, as a matter of fact, that's exactly who I'm going away with!'

'Was going away with,' he amended with arbitrary arrogance.

'And still am!' she flouted, more determined than ever now not to allow him to frustrate her arrangements.

'I doubt it,' Lane disclaimed confidently, shaking his head. 'After all, who has a better right to act as secretary and hostess in my home than my long lost wife?' On an increasingly sarcastic note that abruptly brought a clouded uncertainty to her grey eyes.

'Meaning?'

'Perhaps Sharman would be interested to learn you're still married . . . and to whom!' he threatened meaningfully.

Jenna stared at him, aghast. Fear and anger both vying within her for ascendancy. Eventually, anger won. 'You utterly despicable swine!' she lashed at him witheringly. 'Even blackmail's not too low for an unprincipled mongrel like you to descend to in order to enforce your will, is it?'

'Where my wholly self-centred and perpetually nagging bitch of a wife's concerned, you're so right!' he had no compunction in retorting just as stingingly as his jaw clenched, his expression bleak and derisive. 'Who knows, it could save him a great deal of heartache!'

'Heartache! As if you'd know of any such feeling!' she scoffed in disparaging tones. 'You'd need a heart first before you could experience that emotion, and that's something you've never had, Lane!'

A cynical twist shaped his lips crookedly. 'With you around, my love, it's undoubtedly just as well!'

'Then I'm surprised you're insisting I attend this so-called conference of yours!'

'Because that happens to be business . . . nothing else! Or did you mistakenly think I may have had something more personal in mind as well?' His darkened eyes mocked her silently.

'It wouldn't do you much good even if you had!' she retaliated, a light flush warming her cheeks. 'I know when I'm well off . . . and well out of it!'

'In that case, there's no barrier to your working this weekend, is there?' He returned to their original bone of contention sardonically.

'You mean, now that you've given me notice of your intention to advise Kent of our unfortunate connection if I don't agree?' she gibed.

'Mmm, that's about it,' Lane was not above endorsing. 'Although if you consider our connection so adverse, maybe you should have done something about severing it before this.'

'I was expecting you to!' she flared defensively. 'Besides, I didn't see why I should be put to all that expense. You were the one with all the money.'

'At least some of which I attempted to pass on to you!' he reminded in hard-edged tones. 'I wasn't the one trying to opt out of *my* responsibilities!'

'Well, not any *more* of them, anyway!' Jenna fired back, in spite of a rising feeling of discomfiture. No one was more aware than she was that she had not really done the right thing in leaving him so precipitately, and she could still recall her astonishment when monthly cheques from her husband had begun arriving at her parents' home, her method of departure notwithstanding. Of course she had returned them all, every one of them unopened after the first, whereupon they had not surprisingly eventually stopped arriving altogether, but the fact that he *had* forwarded them had often caused her some moments of disconcertion since.

'Leastways it wasn't all of them!' Lane rapped out explicitly. He paused, breathing deeply, and dragged a hand impatiently through his dark hair. 'Nevertheless, as there's little we can do about that now, and neither of us is likely to gain anything . . .'

'Except for you, of course, by threatening to inform Kent that I'm still married to you!' she interposed bitterly.

'Ah, yes, there is still that, isn't there?' he suddenly smiled so lazily and so attractively that, to her amazement and then mounting annoyance, Jenna experienced a faint stirring of wayward response within her heightened senses. 'But once again, if the situation's so distasteful, perhaps you should have come clean earlier. Or maybe, just to deprive me of the advantage, you could even do so now. I'm sure Sharman would appreciate knowing the truth.' The curve of his lips broadened tauntingly.

Only just managing to suppress the effect his abrupt smile had had on her, Jenna now glared at him in undisguised resentment. Whatever Kent's feelings might be on the matter, she was positive appreciation would not be among them. The more so on discovering just who her husband happened to be! As that goading look on Lane's face proved he was well aware! she seethed.

'As if you care what Kent feels! Your only interest is in making things difficult for me!'

He did not deny it, he just shrugged and pointed out in a drily humorous drawl, 'If I am, you provided me with the means to do so.'

Which was no consolation at all to know! 'Yes—well
. . .' she began, and then came to a sighing halt as a
defeating sense of despondency washed over her.
What was the use of continuing? They were both only
too conscious of who held the upper hand, and it
worried her to think that she may have inadvertently
revealed too much already concerning Kent and
herself. 'I guess it would appear I'll be working this
weekend, then, doesn't it?' A dispirited grimace
twisted her lips as she finally conceded him victory.

'Uh-huh,' Lane confirmed laconically, the satisfied
gleam in his ebony framed, hazel-green eyes not
helping to assuage her already lacerated feelings in the
slightest, and with a dismal nod she took her leave as
quickly as possible.

Her troubled thoughts were somewhat less easy to
leave behind, however, and as she travelled home a
while later a number of them remained aggravatingly
fixed in her mind. That she had unthinkingly supplied
Lane with a way to blackmail her gave her
considerable cause for dismay, but that he would
evidently have no compunction in carrying out his
threat both angered and alarmed her even more. There
was no telling if, or when, he might suddenly decide to
indulge himself by unveiling their relationship, and all
depending on just how he chose to make such a
disclosure, the result could be disastrous as far as she
was concerned!

Stopping at a set of lights, the creases marking
Jenna's forehead deepened fractionally. As well as
that, she recalled, disconcertion had been present
when he had described her in such derogatory terms
too. To her surprise the denunciation had hurt,
although she could not really understand why it

should. She had not retained very endearing memories of him either, so why should it matter what he thought of her?

When she set the car in motion once more, her thoughts moved onwards also. Then again, no less disturbing had been that momentary feeling of attraction a mere smile had succeeded in arousing within her so unexpectedly. She had believed Lane himself had killed any emotions of that nature between them long ago, but to suddenly find them re-surfacing, and at such an incongruous time, not only irritated her but concerned her as well. She did not want to find anything appealing about her husband any more—Kent was the only man who interested her now, wasn't he?—and the knowledge that her senses had responded only made her all the more determined that they would not be permitted to react quite so ungovernably again. Not now that she knew to be on her guard, anyway!

CHAPTER THREE

As anticipated, Kent's response on hearing of Jenna's unavoidable change in plans was a wrathful one. His initial stated intention being for himself to demand of Lane that their arrangements be allowed to stand, but as she was doubtful that would achieve the desired result—as well as extremely apprehensive of the reaction it was more likely to engender!—she was called upon to do some very swift and conciliatory talking in order to dissuade him from such an injudicious course of action.

Not that it seemed to appease him greatly—even though he did finally yield to her reasoning, albeit with ill grace—for he then promptly accused her rancorously of preferring her employer's company to his own, and it took almost as long to disabuse him of that notion as it had the first.

'For heaven's sake, Kent, wherever do you get these ideas?' she half laughed, half frowned, and just a little irritably, when he had eventually calmed down to some degree. It was beginning to nettle her that he should have made such accusations twice now, and especially when nothing could have been further from the truth! 'It's not my fault Lane's called a conference this weekend, and apart from flatly refusing to attend—which no doubt would mean losing my job in consequence—I'm not sure just what you expect me to be able to do about it.'

His blue eyes surveyed her moodily. 'You could

phone on Saturday morning and say you were too ill to go, couldn't you?'

'Oh, yes, I could do that all right,' she agreed on a facetious note. 'Although I can't see anyone believing me when I turn up for work on Monday all nice and tanned after two days on the beach at Woy Woy!'

From his disgruntled expression she gathered even he could recognise the absurdity of that proposal. 'Well, I don't like the idea of you staying the night there! Why can't you go back to your own place on Saturday night and then return again on Sunday?'

'Because it's expected that the conference will probably continue until late on Saturday, and Lane wants to dictate his report early the following day in order to ensure I've enough time to type the final copy that afternoon,' Jenna explained patiently. Then, when he still did not appear particularly mollified. 'Look, I really wasn't all that sold on the idea either when I was informed about it earlier this morning, but if I have to sleep there I can assure you that's all I'll be doing! Sleeping in his house ... not in his bed, if that's what you're thinking!'

'I wouldn't be too sure of that,' he surprised her by disputing with a scowl. 'I've seen the way he watches you at times.'

There could be only one reason for that. 'Probably to see if he can't fault me on something else! He sure doesn't miss me if he can avoid it, believe me!'

'You're saying he's always criticising you?' Kent's brows lifted slightly and then lowered again into a frown. 'You've never mentioned anything about it before.'

'There didn't seem much point,' she shrugged. And particularly when it would have been impossible for her to explain why!

'Then why don't you resign?' he suggested eagerly, looking brighter by the second. 'That way I doubt you'd have to attend his damned conference at all.'

Jenna grimaced wryly. 'That's as may be, but it so happens I don't want to resign, thanks very much. I like it here! Besides, I can't imagine him staying with this company any longer than is absolutely necessary. He must have bigger fish than us to fry, as you once said. So all I figure I have to do is wait him out, and then everything will return to normal,' she gave a hopeful forecast.

'While in the meantime . . .'

'Enduring conferences I'd rather not attend, among other things,' she concluded for him on a sigh, just to make certain he got the right picture.

About to reply, Kent was not given the opportunity when Jenna saw the door to Lane's office starting to open because she waved him away urgently. Jenna had no wish to give her husband cause to vent his displeasure on her for having been found talking to Kent two days in a row. However, their relative proximity still must have afforded Lane some clue, for as he prepared to pass her desk on his way to Ian's office he stopped, his head lowering to within inches of hers.

'I do wish you'd give as much attention to your work as you do to Sharman, my love,' he chided in a goading murmur. 'It could do with some improvement at times.'

Jenna sucked in an irate breath at the deliberate aspersion cast on her proficiency, knowing it to be unwarranted. 'Although not that much that it would excuse me from taking your dictation over the weekend, I gather?' she gritted.

'No, not that much,' he granted so provokingly that she could have kicked him. 'But at the same time it would be appreciated if you could manage to disregard his undoubtedly scintillating presence just a little more often, otherwise you may force me into finding the best way to have him ignoring *you* instead ... and guess what that could involve!' The implied threat, accompanied by an emphasising, chafing tap under her gently rounded chin, was delivered with a smile that did little to diminish its intent, and had her watching his ensuing departure with eyes as stormy as a wind-tossed sea.

Now it was herself that Jenna could have kicked. For not having told Kent the whole truth regarding her marriage while she still had the chance, and thereby permitting Lane to use the knowledge to force her into doing as he wanted whenever it suited him! Oh, yes, he might well look pleased with himself now he had that sword to hold over her head! she smouldered helplessly.

Although by the time Saturday arrived Jenna was no more resigned to the situation than she had been when first told of the proposed conference, she was determined to at least do all in her power to refrain from displaying any such emotion—or any emotion at all, if it came to that, except coolly efficient and businesslike ones—in the hopes of not only ridding Lane of some of the sardonic gratification that had been so much in evidence during the remainder of the

week since she had unwittingly presented him with the
very ammunition he was now able to use against her,
but also to have him deciding that her supposed
indifference would not make it worthwhile to try
something similar again in the future.

With this in mind she set out for his home in plenty
of time to reach it before the designated hour of nine-
thirty while attempting to repress the perturbing, as
well as distressing, thoughts that were already making
themselves felt at the idea of seeing again the house
they had shared together. She made it with a quarter
of an hour to spare, but no matter how hard she tried
to prevent it, a lump still rose in her throat as she
drove up the leafy drive and sat for a moment
contemplating the rustically designed building that
held so many memories. Of course it looked somewhat
different now, for the colour scheme had been
changed, the bush-like gardens re-modelled into a more
formal pattern and the rockery she had filled with
ferns and flowering creepers of every description
disposed of altogether.

Sighing, she shook off such remembrances and made
for the front door with a decisive step, but to her surprise
and no little bewilderment her ring on the bell brought
forth a rather harassed looking young woman with a red
faced and squalling infant held in her arms. It took only a
few minutes of conversation, if a little perplexed on both
sides, to sort the matter out and Jenna shortly returned
to her car feeling extremely foolish. Lane did not live
there any more! Had not done so for some years either,
apparently, because the woman had no recollection of
the name Forrester being that of the previous owner
and, consequently, could not even provide her caller
with a forwarding address.

It had been so automatic on Jenna's part to assume that Lane would have retained their old home, that for a time, as she quickly drove away, she was a little nonplussed as to just what she should do. She now had absolutely no idea as to where he might be living and as he had always had an ex-directory telephone number, even when they had first been married, she doubted a telephone directory would prove to be of much assistance now either. That line of thinking did produce another thought, however, and stopping at the first booth she could find she hurriedly rang Terry Gleeson, Hodgson's office manager, thankfully finding him at home, and even more grateful when he was able to supply the information she needed.

Once armed with the correct address Jenna set off again swiftly. Although both places were north of the city, from Turramurra to Clontarf—a rather exclusive suburb that nestled among the bushy hillside foreshores of Middle Harbour—was still some considerable distance to travel, and with a despairing grimace she knew her intention of arriving calmly and punctually would be well and truly down the drain before she could make it from one to the other.

When she did, it was to find the ribbonstone forecourt of her husband's magnificent two-storeyed, balconied and porticoed residence—it was really too outstanding to be called a mere home, she decided wryly—already well filled with a number of vehicles; and the casually dressed delegates from the various Forrester companies were enjoying a cup of coffee around the sparkling swimming pool set into the terrace just below the house. From where she had just managed to squeeze her small car into a space between two newer and certainly more expensive vehicles,

Jenna only had time to briefly note the full size tennis court located a little further along from the pool and the sleek, shining hulled cabin cruiser swinging gently at its mooring beside the private jetty at the water's edge some distance below, before her attention was caught by a familiar figure approaching her from the pool, two steps at a time.

'You're late! You were supposed to be here over three-quarters of an hour ago!' Lane wasted no time before censuring.

Dressed as informally as the rest of those present his hip-hugging shorts and open weave, knit shirt only seemed to emphasise his essential masculinity and Jenna experienced a momentary sense of confusion.

'I—I'm sorry,' she stammered. 'I did leave in plenty of time but I went to—to the wrong house.'

'How could you have?' His expression registered his disbelief. 'It's not difficult to find!'

Once one knew the right address! Pressing her lips together, she shuffled restively from one foot to the other. 'I—umm—didn't realise you'd moved,' she relayed in a self-conscious mumble.

'From where?' he frowned. Followed by an incredulously comprehending, 'You mean, from Turramurra?' He uttered a short, disparaging sound. 'You thought I'd want to remain in that house with all the disagreeable memories if contained?'

'No, I suppose not,' she agreed tautly. She guessed she would not have wanted to remain either if their positions had been reversed, although she still did not consider there was any necessity for him to be quite so derisive about it. 'I just didn't think.'

'You never did!' he charged. 'At least, not about anything more important than which invitation to accept next!' He paused. 'Not that I've the time or the inclination to be discussing that now. We're already late getting started, thanks to you. So where's your case?' His brows peaked above coolly enquiring eyes.

'Still in my car,' she advised, moving to open the door, and doing her best not to answer his condemnation in kind.

'My God! Do you mean that death-trap's yours?' Lane exclaimed disgustedly behind her as she extracted her one small piece of luggage from the dilapidated vehicle. 'Can't you do better than that?'

Closing the door again, Jenna turned back to face him with a deprecating shrug. 'It serves its purpose.'

'The only purpose that looks capable of serving is as an addition to a junk yard!' The disdainful curve of his mouth became more apparent as he took her case from her and began heading for the house. 'How on earth do you get it passed for registration? By making eyes at the mechanic while he's supposed to be checking it over?' He sent her a jeering look over one shoulder.

'No!' Her eyes flashed angrily at his broad back. 'It's a struggle sometimes, but I've managed so far without resorting to such tactics!'

'You surprise me!'

Jenna clamped her teeth together and refused to give him the satisfaction of offering another word in her car's defence. What concern was it of his what the condition the vehicle she drove was in, anyway! Besides, she was having enough trouble keeping up with his long-legged stride as it was, without trying to concentrate on such an irrelevant conversation too.

Crossing the tiled porch they passed the open, heavy oak front door and entered a wide, lace grille-enclosed foyer, although there was very little time for Jenna to observe her surroundings to any extent for she was immediately shown through one such delicately constructed door into a hallway at the same rapid pace and, after mounting a flight of curving, thickly carpeted stairs, finally into a large, high-ceilinged bedroom complete with sliding glass doors leading on to a balcony overlooking the harbour. However, not even here was she allowed more than a moment to glance around before Lane had deposited her case at the end of a sprigged lilac and white quilted bed and she was being hustled back down the stairs again with only a vague impression of light coloured furniture, a highly polished floor, and lilac curtains at the windows left in her mind.

On reaching the ground floor once more, Lane's stride seemed to lengthen even more, so that the room they passed appeared little more than a blur to Jenna, her only impression now one of understated luxury and uncluttered airiness. Their destination this time she discovered was the kitchen—a bright, ultra-modern, space saving room—where she was perfunctorily introduced to Enid Squires, Lane's middle-aged and somewhat reserved housekeeper. Leastways, reserved towards herself that was, she noticed idly, for the woman's attitude towards her employer was quite easy and unconstrained.

'Would you care for a cup of coffee, Miss Bowman?' the housekeeper now enquired politely, but still with that hint of restrained formality. 'I have some already brewing.'

Jenna nodded appreciatively. 'Thank you, that would be . . .'

'Sorry, there isn't time for that,' Lane broke in summarily to override her acceptance, and already starting to urge her out of the kitchen by another door. 'You'll have to wait until we break for morning tea.' Adding for the housekeeper's benefit as they left the room. 'At about eleven-thirty now, I suppose, Enid, since we're starting late.'

This time Jenna did have something to say— indignantly. After all, enough was enough! 'I could have at least taken it with me, couldn't I?' she demanded, shaking off the disturbing hand that had been impelling her along by the nape of her neck.

'So you could clatter and clink all through the first session? No, thanks! If you're thirsty you can have some of the iced water that is already on the table.' Lane nodded to indicate the bedewed carafes already reposing on the long oval table that took pride of place in the room they had just entered.

Jenna took stock swiftly. Noting the individual folders containing the agenda for the conference as well as various papers imparting other pertinent information that she had typed during the week already placed around the table, together with an array of writing pads, pens, pencils, glasses and ashtrays.

'You're sure you can trust me not to spill it all over everything?' she glanced upwards to snipe sarcastically.

'I hope so . . . for your sake.' He returned her gaze mockingly. 'You could find it difficult trying to take notes and clean up the mess at the same time.'

In other words, she should not expect any tolerance whatsoever, she deduced with a grimace, and sighing, looked back at the table. 'Where do I sit?' she asked flatly.

'Right beside me, naturally!' Not a little tauntingly. 'Where else?'

Where else, indeed, since he no doubt intended to be as critical here as he was in the office! 'And my notebooks and pencils?'

'In the office—through here,' he relayed, making for a smaller, adjoining room.

Jenna followed him gloomily. She was beginning to suspect the weekend was going to be even less pleasant than she had imagined. Although on seeing the office her spirits did rise a little. As with the rest of the house it was certainly an agreeably designed room and the equipment therein the latest in design. Why, even the typewriter was an electronic one rather than just an electric one like she used at the office; the copying machine and telex obviously both recent models even if not quite as large as those installed at Hodgson's.

'You've used one of those before?' Lane queried, gesturing towards the typewriter.

She shook her head. 'No, although I don't expect it will take me long to learn. There is an instruction manual that came with it, I presume?'

'Mmm, in one of the desk drawers, I believe.' Sounds began filtering through from the conference room and he turned to leave. 'You'd better leave it until afterwards to look for it, though. It seems everyone's anxious to begin ... now we're here at last.'

Ignoring yet another of his apparently irresistible digs at her failure to arrive on time—no matter how unintentional it may have been—Jenna merely dropped her shoulder bag into an empty filing tray and, collecting a notebook and a number of well sharpened pencils, returned to the conference room in his wake.

Although most of the men present obviously knew

each other relatively well, Jenna was acquainted with none of them, even by sight, apart from Lane and Ian Leonard, though she had spoken to a couple over the phone, and the brief introductions performed by her husband did not exactly fill her with confidence at being able to match the correct name to the various statements made once they got down to business.

In this regard, though, Lane proved to be more understanding than she had expected, and certainly more than he had previously indicated, for by virtue of her chair being set so close to his, he would lean across and helpfully recall for her each man's name when they began to speak. There were also other instances when he signalled that it was not necessary for her to make any notes at all, and during one of these periods she had the chance to study those attending a little more thoroughly.

As Kent had once predicted, it appeared very few of them, except for Ian and maybe one or two of the others, would have reached the age of forty. An almost opposite arrangement to the hierarchy under the old regime at Hodgson Industries, she noted. To a man they were also earnest, enthusiastic, alert, and ... smart! she soon came to realise on observing their quick assimilation of any problems that may have arisen, followed by a seemingly even more readily devised variety of methods suitable for either circumventing or disposing of any such drawbacks altogether.

It was also a setting she had never witnessed her husband in before, and as the meeting progressed she found herself listening to his suggestions and comments with increasing interest. That he knew his subject was indisputable; his employees' respect for that knowledge just as evident in their attitude of genuine attentiveness when he spoke, and their appreciation of his courtesy in always hearing their own proposals and remarks out without interruption. Another point that came through noticeably was that Lane was obviously well-liked by his staff too, and she wondered if that was one of the reasons that accounted for each of them, apparently quite willingly, giving up half their weekend in order to participate in a business conference.

So occupied was she with her own thoughts that it took a while for Jenna to realise that Lane was motioning, somewhat impatiently by then, for her to continue taking notes again and with a guilty start she dropped her gaze hastily to her book, her pencil flying across the page furiously in an effort to record all that had been said.

When next she was granted another of those periodic pauses it was while Lane himself was discussing a side issue with a couple of the men from head office, and unaccountably Jenna felt her glance being drawn to his face and for an even less understandable reason allowed it to remain there, though surreptitiously. He had an arresting profile, she mused. The planes and curves thus viewed not only reflecting a surface ruggedness but an inner resolve as well somehow. His forehead was wide and intelligent, his sable lashed eyes expressive and capable of making a woman feel as if her very bones were melting, as she knew from experience, his firm and attractively shaped mouth impossible to ignore when it curved with sudden laughter—as it was doing now in response to some evidently humorous remark. Abruptly assaulted by an overwhelming rush of instinctive magnetism she could not subdue, Jenna bit at her lip in a panic, her wide grey eyes stricken with dismay. The more so when Lane chose that moment to slant his gaze in her direction.

Immediately his brows snapped together in curious speculation. 'What's wrong?' he probed under cover of the continuing conversation around the table.

'Oh—er—nothing,' she denied throatily, looking everywhere but at him. 'It was just a—a touch of cramp in my leg, I think.'

'Do you want to walk around for a bit?'

Why did he have to pick now to show some concern? 'No, no—it seems to have gone now, anyway.'

'Well, we'll be breaking for morning tea shortly. You can give it some exercise then.'

Jenna simply nodded and determinedly returned her attention to the pad resting on her crossed knee. In fact, she did not look up again until they did finally call a halt for some refreshment, and then only reluctantly. It was not exercise she needed, she sighed despairingly. It was an effective means to curb those strangely unpredictable, and perturbingly unruly feelings of physical appeal she experienced with regard to her husband at times!

With only another three breaks during the remainder of the day, the meeting continued in much the same fashion, although after dinner that evening it seemed to Jenna that her duties included more dispensing of drinks than the taking of notes, as the discussions became less specifically related to the agenda. By ten the conference had been wound up completely and after the delegates had offered their friendly farewells she retired to the office to begin transcribing her shorthand, and was well into it by the time Lane returned from seeing the last of the men away some thirty minutes later.

'You don't have to do that now. In the morning will do,' he declared from the doorway where he leant negligently against the wall, watching her.

'I may as well get some of it done,' she shrugged. 'It's too early to go to bed.'

The corners of his mouth sloped mockingly. 'All depending on the reason you go there, of course.'

Jenna flushed, but refused to be drawn as she worried apprehensively whether there had been an inferred suggestion in his remark.

'You're finding the typewriter no problem, then?' His following question was so matter-of-fact that it had her grimacing ruefully at her own implausible thinking. Naturally he was not interested in having anything to do with her on a personal level! Why would he be? Especially when he had the obviously all too willing Rosalind to fulfil his every desire! the slightly niggling thought followed.

'No, it's great once you become used to the additional functions,' she finally answered lightly.

'Right! Well, I'll leave you to it in peace.' Lane pushed himself upright again. 'I'll be out for the rest of the evening,' with the fair Rosalind no doubt! deduced Jenna tartly, 'but if there's anything you want, just ask Enid, and I'll see you at breakfast on the patio in the morning.'

She nodded, his mention of his housekeeper reminding her of a thought she had been intermittently puzzling over all day, and as he turned to leave she called after him tentatively. 'Lane . . .'

'Mmm . . .?' He only partly swung back to face her.

She took a deep breath. 'Does Mrs Squires know we're married?'

He flexed one shoulder indifferently. 'I haven't told her we are, if that's what you mean.' Then, with a slight frown as he faced her squarely, 'What makes you ask?'

'She treats me with so much more reserve than she does everyone else, and—and I just wondered . . .'

'If she was siding with me over our separation?' he voiced her suspicions wryly, and then gave a dismissive laugh. 'It's probably because she only met you for the first time today. She's known the others much longer.'

That was what Jenna had convinced herself earlier too, except . . . 'Not Ian, though, but I noticed she was calling him by his first name most of the day.'

'Well, don't take it to heart,' he recommended drily with another unconcerned hunching of his shoulders. 'Maybe she figured you had enough impressed admirers here today without her adding to their number. You can't expect to have everyone falling at your feet, you know.'

As if she did! But that acid sting in his last words certainly seemed to resolve another point she had found herself pondering during the day. From the dissatisfied look she had observed on his face at times she had suspected he had not been at all enamoured of her affable popularity with his staff, although just why, she could not fathom. It definitely had not interfered with his conference in any way!

With his departure, Jenna resumed her typing, but not before giving vent to an inward self-mocking laugh for her earlier wariness in thinking he may have wanted something more from her than mere secretarial ability. She was becoming as fanciful as Kent!

The sky was already blue when Jenna woke in the morning, and unable to resist the view from her balcony she padded across to it pleasurably. Even at that relatively early hour the harbour was adorned with a variety of leisure craft and yachts—some displaying gay multi-coloured sails, others just dazzling white ones—that skimmed across the glistening blue water as far as the eye could see. She could have stayed there soaking up the sunshine and the panoramic scene for some time, but the clink of glass and china coming from somewhere below her had her reluctantly remembering the reason for her presence in the house and she re-entered the room with a sigh.

Presently, after washing and changing into a pair of slim fitting, dusty blue denims and a bright red, stretch knit top, she made her way down the stairs and on to the patio where she discovered Lane to have almost finished his breakfast.

'I'm sorry,' she apologised awkwardly on taking the seat across from him at the white lace and glass-topped table. 'I—I'd forgotten how early you always liked to eat in the mornings.'

'No sweat,' he discounted lazily, a provoking smile pulling at his lips. 'I hadn't forgotten how you prefer to wake slowly ... sometimes.'

He was meaning those times early in their marriage when she had had no objections at all to waking swiftly if it meant him making love to her again, Jenna knew, and her creamy cheeks flamed with embarrassment. 'Yes—well—thankfully I can wake as late as I please nowadays,' she tried to inject a little protective taunting into her own words.

The green of Lane's eyes was conspicuously visible for a second and then it disappeared. 'Sharman's not an early riser either?' he surmised sardonically.

On the verge of hotly repudiating his disagreeable insinuation, she abruptly decided against it. Since he had made it no secret that he considered such affairs quite acceptable for himself, why shouldn't she claim the same also? She slanted him a mocking look from beneath curling lashes.

'No, as a matter of fact, he's not,' she conceded in dulcet tones, and quite truthfully, for whenever they had stayed with Kent's parents he had always been the last to make it to the breakfast table. 'Still I suppose that's not altogether surprising. We're up late most nights . . . talking.' With just enough of an evocatively smiled delay to have him believing it was something entirely other than speech that kept them awake.

Apparently she was successful in her aim too, because it was almost possible to hear Lane's teeth snap as his jaw clenched. 'Then you must get along together just fine,' he gibed on a grating note.

'Yes, we do,' she endorsed complacently, helping herself to toast from the rack already on the table, and not at all averse to adding a little more fuel to the fire. So he didn't like the idea of his wife having an affair. Well, wasn't that just too bad! And particularly since it was unquestionably his ego that had suffered a blow at the belief, certainly not his ethics!

'Although not quite well enough, evidently, to have you wanting to marry him.' A decidedly more subtle inflection edged some of the abrasiveness out of his voice.

Jenna's eyes flickered warily. She knew that silky nuance of old—and the astute brain that had produced it. 'What makes you think that?'

'In the main, the fact that you haven't yet sought a divorce, I guess,' he relayed, his expression openly mocking now. 'Plus your obviously being unwilling to even tell him you're not free to marry again, of course.'

'I'm not unwilling to tell him,' she denied, valiantly attempting to outface him. 'I—I'm just not *ready* to do so at the moment, that's all.'

'And never will be without that divorce, will you, my pet?'

The goading amusement in his tone was too much for Jenna to bear and her chin lifted rebelliously. 'Then I'll just have to instigate proceedings in order to get one, won't I?'

'I wouldn't recommend it,' he drawled.

'And why not?'

'Because I shall fight it every inch of the way. You forget, *I'm* quite content with matters the way they are.' His lips twitched wryly. 'It saves unnecessary complications.'

'Well, that's just great for you, isn't it?' she flared, sarcasm uppermost. 'But I couldn't happen to care less about your *complications*! We've lived apart for the required number of years so there's nothing you can do to prevent me from getting a judgment on the grounds of separation.'

'Except that for those grounds *both* parties have to be agreeable, and naturally I shall claim to have repented of my unacceptable ways and to be only waiting for the chance to begin again with my dearly beloved wife.'

'You w-wouldn't?' She did not know whether such a contention would be sufficient to deprive her of a divorce, but she did surmise it could be sufficient to make it a forbiddingly expensive and drawn out exercise.

'Why don't you put it to the test and we'll see, hmm?' he suggested tauntingly, smugly, as he rose lithely to his feet. 'Meanwhile, though . . .' his teeth flashed in an intolerably aggravating smile, 'don't be too long in typing up those notes, will you? I'd like to get down to dictating my report as soon as possible.'

Jenna would have liked to have volubly consigned both him and his report to hell, and only by hastily gritting her teeth did she avoid doing so. 'You're sure you can spare me the time for breakfast?' she sniped astringently instead.

'Oh, I think so,' he averred indolently. 'After all, I wouldn't want you to think yourself too hard done by.' And with another intolerably provoking smile he left the patio, whistling.

In other words, after winning all the major points he had no objection to being big-hearted on the small ones! she supposed with a disgruntled grimace, and set about spreading her toast with a furiously wielded knife.

Once started, it did not take Jenna much more than an hour or so to finish with her notes due to the amount she had managed to do the night before, and then after a short wait while Lane scanned the typed pages swiftly and made a few notations of his own, she was back to recording once more as he started dictating his report and associated recommendations.

Thankfully, this was not quite as lengthy as she had anticipated, and after a short and somewhat silent halt for lunch (she was still too wrathfully resentful at his threat to contest any divorce proceedings she might instigate, to even want to acknowledge his presence, let alone engage in any conversation), it was eventually completed early in the afternoon. Just in time to allow him to speak leisurely with haughty Rosalind on taking her call in the office, noted Jenna sourly as she inserted paper into the typewriter, and wishing perversely that it was a manual machine. The noisy clatter would have done much to provide an outlet for her vexed feelings, as well as probably forced him to continue his sickeningly indulgent conversation elsewhere!

When he finally replaced the receiver, Lane crossed to her desk but Jenna ignored him, pretending to be engrossed in reading her shorthand. That was until a strong brown hand was deliberately placed on her pad, effectively hiding everything from view.

'Did you want something?' She did look up now, with facetiously widening eyes.

His firmly moulded lips pulled into an ironic line. 'Only to advise that I'm going out.'

'Okay,' she shrugged her indifference—why should it matter to her if he could not keep away from the woman?—and returned her gaze meaningfully to the hand still resting on her notebook.

A look that was resolutely disregarded. 'So how long do you expect to be on the report?'

'A couple of hours or so, I guess,' she made her answer purposely vague. Since he would not be there, it could mean she would be able to get away early if she completed it in less time.

'Well, you'd still better wait until I return,' he unknowingly—or was it? wondered Jenna suspiciously on glaring upwards involuntarily and finding him with a bantering smile curving his mouth—put paid to her hopes. 'I'd like to check it through before all the copies are made.'

In that case, why couldn't he forgo the dubious pleasure of seeing his disdainful girl-friend for once? she fumed. 'So how long do *you* expect to be, then?' she all but demanded.

'I couldn't say for certain. Just expect me when you see me,' he recommended in a nonchalant drawl as he executed a sketchy salute and turned for the door.

Momentarily, Jenna sent a fulminating glare winging after him, then with a heavily expelled sigh returned her attention to the work at hand. At present there was really very little she could do to alleviate the one-sided situation except keep in mind the consoling thought that it could not last for ever. Lane would have to take up his position at head office again some time, and then ... and then, she smiled pleasurably, she would be able to get on with her own life once again without any more of his arbitrary interference. Also, her thoughts moved on in the same hopeful fashion, once they were out of each other's sight again he could quite possibly have second thoughts about obstructing her gaining a divorce.

With this fortifying idea fixed firmly in her mind, she felt more relaxed and able to resume typing in a much less turbulent state. The result being that she finished the report even faster than she had expected, but after checking it, conversely found herself with nothing to do and all her previous sense of indignation recurring as she waited less than patiently for Lane to return.

Of course, if she had thought to bring a costume with her she could have made use of the pool, she mused fractiously, but as she had not that was not an avenue she could utilise to relieve either her increasing boredom or irritation. Eventually, after having explored the whole of the terraced grounds and the jetty for want of something better to do, she made use of her husband's video library at Enid Squires' suggestion. It was better than doing nothing and for a while at least it did succeed in taking her mind off her enforced inactivity, but when Lane still had not put in an appearance by seven o'clock, she decided she had had enough and after collecting her already packed case from upstairs went in search of his housekeeper.

'I'm leaving now, Mrs Squires,' she advised almost defiantly. 'I've some things to do at home and I'd like to get them done before midnight, if possible.'

'Oh, but I thought ...' The greying haired woman began, and then stopped to indicate the pots already on the kitchen's island hotplates. 'Lane did say he'd be back in time for dinner, you know.'

'Mmm, but for tonight's ... or tomorrow's?' Jenna quipped drily.

'It *is* getting a little late, I must admit,' came the surprisingly half smiled return. 'But I'm sure he won't be much longer.'

Jenna was not nearly so confident! 'Yes, well, I still think I'll be going all the same,' she refused to alter her decision. 'It's beginning to get dark and I prefer not to drive my car at night if I can avoid it. The headlights aren't always as reliable as they might be, I'm afraid.' Her soft lips shaped ruefully.

'Oh, in that case perhaps you had better leave,' the housekeeper nodded with concern. 'I'll explain to Lane when he returns.'

'Thank you,' Jenna smiled gratefully, a little relieved too. There was no guarantee she would have trouble with her lights tonight, of course, but it could prove to be a handy excuse, especially if forwarded by an impartial third party.

Leaving the house with a brisk, and somewhat triumphant step a short while later, Jenna swiftly stowed her case on the back seat of the Volkswagen before taking her place in the front and, switching the ignition on, sighed expressively on discovering her lights to be working. There had not been any guarantee they *would* work tonight either! However, she had only just reversed from where she had been parked and was starting down the drive when she was confronted by two brightly blazing beams on a vehicle turning into the property, the ensuring arrogant blast on the horn of the approaching Alpha Romeo informing her of the driver's identity as adequately as any words could have done.

So he had finally condescended to return, had he? she scowled, and railed against the fates who had decreed he could not have been just a few minutes later as she brought her car to a halt with grimacing reluctance.

Lane pulled up alongside, their open windows in line. 'I thought I told you to wait until I got back!' he rapped out authoritatively.

'So you did,' she acceded on a smouldering note. 'But how was I to know how long your girl-friend's scintillating company,' remembering his similarly sardonic comment about Kent, 'would hold you spellbound? For all I was aware you could have decided not to come back tonight at all!'

His expressive brows peaked mockingly. 'What, when I knew my beautiful and delightfully co-operative wife was just awaiting my return with undoubtedly bated breath? How could I possibly pass up such pleasure?'

'It would be the first time you didn't, then!' she snapped. 'And don't keep calling me your wife! I haven't been that for years!'

'Well, maybe not in a physical sense,' he owned, but in such a lazily evocative voice that she could not prevent a self-conscious flush from warming her cheeks. 'Although in every other respect you definitely are, my love.'

Did he have to keep reminding her? 'And you can stop calling me "your love" so sarcastically too!' she directed fierily. It was really the only point he had left for her to dispute.

'You'd rather I said it with more appropriate ardour?'

His undisguised amusement had her temper flaring. 'No! I'd rather you didn't use it at all!' She paused, inhaling deeply, and slanted him a long taunting look from under glossy lashes. 'Or I just might be tempted to return the favour and start calling you *"my* love", or even "sweetheart", in your avid Miss Cornell's presence.'

Lane hunched one shoulder unconcernedly. 'You could, of course, although I somehow doubt it would worry Rosalind greatly.'

Because she was so sure of his interest in her? speculated Jenna acrimoniously. 'It might, though, if she should suddenly discover just *who* you're married to,' she threatened slyly. If it was acceptable for him to blackmail her, why should she be backward in using identical methods against him?

'Quite possibly,' he conceded with an utterly indifferent laugh. 'But if you think that's likely to cause me any lost sleep, my love,' he used the term deliberately, goadingly, 'then you're wasting your time, believe me. *You're* the one who's nervous of people discovering you're still married, not me. You can tell who you like for all I care, although you do realise, of course, that the more who know, the more likely it is that word will get back to Sharman.'

Unfortunately he was probably right, Jenna admitted grudgingly and gave a despondent sigh. So once again Lane had won another round. The situation was becoming more biased in his direction by the day! She decided a change of topic could be prudent—before she lost any more ground!

'Well, now that you *have* returned, do you want to check that report or not?'

'That was my intention.' He inclined his head briefly, sardonically, and set off in the purring Alpha for the garage.

Jenna did not bother to turn her own vehicle again but began reversing towards the house, the abrupt flickering of her headlights advising her that even her car was not about to allow her a victory today.

'So what's up with your car?' Lane questioned immediately she joined him at the front steps.

'Nothing,' she contended. Trust him to have seen!

'You mean, the lights play up like that all the time?' caustically.

'No, not all the time.' Jenna's tone became defensive. 'Just sometimes.'

As they walked into the house his eyes swept over her satirically. 'Then don't you think it might be an idea to have them fixed?'

'I've tried to!' she retorted. 'But the problem just seems to keep reappearing. The car's just getting old, I guess.'

'*Getting* old?' He uttered a short, mirthless bark of

explicit laughter. 'It should have been reduced to scrap years ago!'

'Well, it wasn't, and if you'd returned at a decent hour I wouldn't be needing to use the lights in order to get home!'

'You won't, anyway!' he stated categorically. 'I'll be taking you home in my car after that exhibition of its capabilities!'

'No, you will not!' she rounded on him indignantly. Was there no end to his overbearing dictates? As she recalled, he had not even been this autocratic during the time they had lived together!

'*Yes, I will!*' The line of his jaw hardened as his darkening eyes locked relentlessly with hers.

As much as Jenna would have liked to have doggedly refused to submit, not only did his determined expression warn her of the probable futility of such an action, but the knowledge that she was not looking forward to the drive if there was a chance her lights might fail on the way, combined to defeat her, and her shoulders slumped resignedly.

'I—well—I still can't see why it was so imperative that you read the report tonight, in any event,' she complained moodily. 'Surely it wouldn't have made that much difference to have checked it in the office in the morning.'

'Save for the fact that I won't *be* in the office tomorrow,' Lane retorted, a lingering sting still in his tone. 'I'm flying down to Melbourne at seven-thirty and don't expect to be back until some time on Tuesday.'

'Oh!' It was the first she had been told of it. 'Well, it would be nice if you could manage to inform me of all these arrangements a little earlier instead of always springing them on me at the last moment!' she flashed more spiritedly as they entered the office.

'In order to make it easier for you to plan your time with Sharman?'

'Among other things,' she concurred, her voice no less crackling than his own. 'But if I'm supposed to be your secretary then I should have been informed, and why wasn't I the one to make your flight bookings, anyway?'

'Because I considered you had enough to keep you occupied last week so I asked Flora to book them for me instead.'

Ah, yes, his co-operative permanent secretary! she recollected, her lips twisting. 'And would there happen to be any other such plans in the offing that I might be permitted to know about?' Her winged brows arched satirically.

Having seated himself casually on a corner of her desk and picked up the report, he now eyed her blandly above the neatly typed pages. 'I'll let you know at the appropriate time,' he drawled before dropping his gaze to the papers he was holding.

Jenna swung away irritably and went to stand by the window, unseeing of the light-spangled panorama outside, her previous suspicion becoming more of a certainty now. For some perverse reason known only to himself, he *was* trying to make things as difficult as possible for her with Kent! she seethed. But why? That was what she could not comprehend. Okay, so he obviously had not taken to the idea of her supposedly being on more intimate terms with Kent than she actually was, but his obstructiveness had started before any mention of that had been made. Her forehead creased contemplatively. Unless, of course, it

was just that their marriage had left him with such a
dislike of her that he was willing to use any means at
his disposal to exact his revenge. It was an abruptly
discomforting thought, and she unconsciously half
turned to view the subject of her depressing musings.

That was something else that baffled her too, she
frowned. Just why his animosity should appear to have
the power to cause those unexpected stabs of pain.
Annoyance, maybe, but surely not hurt? After all, it
was not as if she cared for him any more, despite that
flagrantly male attraction of his succeeding in
penetrating her defences on occasion—and in a way
Kent never had, the ensuing comparison came
unbidden and was suppressed in a panic. Staunchly
she continued her covert scrutiny, only to have her
memories work against her as she found herself
wondering if his sensuous mouth was still as
tantalisingly persuasive, his long-fingered hands as
skilfully arousing, his ultimate love-making as . . .
With a horrified gasp for the course of her wayward
thoughts, and as a rosy glow climbed up to her
cheekbones, she frantically brought the mortifying
reverie to a halt.

'Well . . .?' The sudden query had her swallowing
heavily and the colour tinting her cheeks deepening on
realising Lane was sardonically returning her appraising gaze.

'I—umm—was just thinking,' she stammered with a
treacherous huskiness.

'Somewhat heatedly, it would seem.'

Jenna chewed at her lip in dismay. He could not
possibly have guessed the perturbing nature of her
thoughts, could he? 'I guess you—you could say that,'
she somehow managed to shrug deprecatingly.

'And since those eloquent eyes of yours were focused squarely on myself, it would not take much to surmise just whom all that intense emotion was directed against, would it?'

Thank God he believed it had been against, and not *about* him! she almost sagged in relief. It gave her the encouragement to gibe bittersweetly, 'Yes, well, you may be in a position to exert some control over my actions at the moment, Lane, but my thoughts are still wholly my own to command!'

'As are mine, my love!' he mocked incisively. 'And when they concern you, you can take my word for it that they're certainly no less vehement!'

'I didn't expect it to be otherwise,' she claimed, her facial muscles aching in her effort to appear unaffected. And in the hope of diverting him, nodded towards the report. 'Does it pass? Because if so, I'd like to get the copying done as soon as possible, and if not, I'd like to make any corrections as soon as possible.'

'It passes,' he advised curtly, thrusting it towards her. 'Although you needn't bother with the copies now,' as she made for the relevant machine, 'you can take it with you and do them at the office tomorrow.' A brief pause and he went on at his most sarcastic, 'That is what you would prefer, isn't it?'

And when had that ever concerned him before? Not that she was about to air any grievances now, though. She simply nodded an affirming, 'Of course.'

'Right!' Lane rose to his feet fluidly, swiftly. Almost as if he was now as anxious for her to depart as she had been previously, Jenna pondered in surprise, and some puzzlement. 'Then let's go, shall we?'

With a half shrugged, half nodded consent, she preceded him from the room, her mind whirling in confusion. Now what had she done to create such a heightening of the tension between them? Made out her thoughts of him had not been very pleasant ones? But he already knew that! Shaking her head imperceptibly, she released a small sigh as they left the house. She supposed she should have felt some sort of elation at having apparently riled him for a change—even if she was not aware as to just how she had accomplished it—but inexplicably she did not. She just felt tense, tired, and even a little bit tearful she abruptly realised in astonishment as her eyes suddenly misted. Luckily, Lane was fetching her case while she waited beside his dark blue Alpha and so she was able to hastily blink them clear before he returned, but even so kept her head downbent when he opened the door for her.

'Wh-what about my car?' she still had to ask as they passed it on the driveway, although she would rather have remained silent, the throaty quality present in her voice causing her some disquiet. 'I'll need it to—to get to work tomorrow.'

'I'll have Floyd, Enid's husband, run it over to the plant some time during the day. You'll have to make do with public transport in the morning,' he clipped out carelessly.

'Thank you.' Her acknowledgment was faintly made.

'What, no recriminations for having deprived you of it at all?' His goading still contained a cutting edge that was all too successful in its intent.

'No.' Jenna averted her gaze by turning to stare blindly through the side window this time as her eyes blurred uncontrollably again. 'Just thankful that I don't have to make the trip all the way out to Clontarf by public transport in order to collect it myself,' she tried to quip, but it came out on too quavering a note to be particularly effective.

Having evidently anticipated something far more pungent, Lane slanted her a raking glance, but as this only connected with a silky fall of sun-bleached hair due to her carefully concealing position, he gave a dismissive shrug and they continued on their way in silence.

For Jenna the journey seemed to take even longer than it had for her the morning before, although she knew it obviously had not if only because of the reduced number of vehicles on the road, but she had still never felt more relieved than when they finally came to a halt outside her apartment building. In fact, she had released her seatbelt and was pushing open her door almost before the car had stopped.

'Jenna . . .?' Lane leant across from his own seat to call after her as she scrambled to her feet on the pavement.

Was that a note of anxiety she could detect in his voice? she speculated as she turned to shut the door. Then laughed mutely, mockingly, at herself for having such a freakish imagination. 'Thank you for the lift—good night,' she interposed hurriedly before he had an opportunity to say anything more and, about-facing, rushed into the building and up to her small apartment as swiftly as her slightly unsteady legs would carry her.

Once inside, she sank back against the door weakly, her determinedly repressed tears now beginning to fall unchecked—until an imperative rap on the door had her jumping away from it with a start.

'Go away, Lane!' she ordered chokingly through

the thinly veneered wood, guessing her caller's identity.

In response, there was an even more thunderous knocking, and alarmed in case it brought out all the other tenants to see what the commotion was about, she reluctantly opened the door, but only barely.

'Go away, Lane!' she repeated to his face now, on finding her assumption had been correct.

'I thought you may have wanted this.' An ironical tilt caught at his mouth as he indicated her case resting on the floor beside him.

'Oh!' She stared down at it self-consciously. Then wanting only to escape his presence, made a hasty move to pick it up. 'I—I'm sorry. Thank you for bringing it up.'

Lane's hand was far faster than hers, however. He was already lifting it before her fingers could reach it, and pushing the door wider he calmly entered the apartment as if he had every right to be there. 'Where do you want it put?' he turned to enquire.

'Anywhere!' She gestured becoming flustered.

Shrugging, he deposited it beside a slightly threadbare sofa and then retraced his steps to the door, but not in order to leave as Jenna had hoped, but to push it shut with one hand while unexpectedly turning her face up to his with the other.

'You *were* crying in the car,' he declared as if proving something to himself.

As there had been no opportunity to either blink or wipe away the betraying evidence, there did not seem much point in denying it. 'In relief at—at knowing the weekend was f-finally over,' she attempted another quip instead, but it failed even more miserably than her last and she had to press her lips together tightly to stop their traitorous trembling.

He smiled at that, but it was such a warm, captivating, and completely natural widening of his shapely mouth that Jenna could not have taken exception to it even if it had not had her breath catching waywardly in her throat, and then his demeanour reverted to a more thoughtfully assessing mien.

'I'm sorry,' he surprised her both by apologising and the gentleness with which his fingers smoothed away the dampness from her cheeks. 'But you crowd me so much at times that . . .' He broke off, exhaling deeply, and rubbed a hand roughly round the back of his neck. 'I guess just knowing we *are* still married tends to arouse certain instincts, whether we like it or not.'

In other words, she had been reduced to tears all because his punctured male pride was suffering! she deduced bitterly, scornfully. It was enough to have her squaring her shoulders and pulling resentfully away from the hand that still rested casually beneath her softly rounded chin.

'Then perhaps you should re-consider your proposed objection to our becoming divorced!' she asserted heatedly.

'Uh-uh!' The smile that accompanied his laconic, but decisive veto was deceptive. Initially amused, then next, insufferably taunting. 'It provides me with a considerable amount of satisfaction to have you dancing to my tune for a change, my pet, in return for those hellish years you gave me.' The green of his eyes glinted with lazy goading. 'In any case, even if you did marry Sharman, you'd regret it within a month. You're no more compatible than . . .'

'You and I were?' she inserted in caustic accents. Those years had been hellish for her too! But how dared he presume to judge her and Kent's relationship!

'Even less!' Lane shot back derisively.

Jenna's finely formed features clouded with stormy indignation. 'Well, that's for me to find out! It has nothing whatsoever to do with you, that's for sure!' And pulling open the door again, she inclined her head towards it meaningfully. 'So now, if you don't mind ... I do believe I have *some* rights in my own home!'

'Of course,' he drawled and, to her relief, began moving towards the opening she had provided. 'Although I wouldn't be too ready to disclaim any interest, or *influence*,' graphically stressed, 'on my behalf concerning your little affair, if I were you, or I may be tempted to prove just how wrong you are.'

'I know! I know! By telling Kent about our marriage!' she jeered disparagingly.

'Not ... necessarily.' The cryptic assertion had a sudden wary frown descending on to her forehead as he passed her. 'There's more than one way to disrupt your amorous activities, you know,' he added on a complacent, rankling note.

And if it suited him, he undoubtedly would not be averse to using any of them—whatever they were! The thought was so infuriating to contemplate that it had her shaking with the force of her rising emotions.

'Just get out, Lane!' she gritted between clenched teeth. 'And stay out of my life too!'

'When I feel like it, maybe I will, but until then ...' He flexed a wide shoulder expressively, and stepped into the hallway.

Jenna slammed the door resoundingly after him, her feelings smouldering out of control. And to think she had allowed him to upset her to the extent of crying! she cursed herself roundly for having been so weak. But at least she was recovering some of her senses now, she was pleased to note, and knowing that a good night's sleep would only improve them more, she felt confident of waking in the morning with her spirits fully restored.

Nevertheless, Lane's last threat did cause her some moments of concern as she lay in bed later, and for a time it had her tossing and turning restlessly. Of course the only way to destroy his major hold over her was to tell Kent the whole truth, but as that seemed out of the question while Lane remained with Hodgson's—Kent himself having permanently settled that with all his unwarranted suspicions, she recalled vexedly—she could not quite see how she could overcome the problem.

Unless . . . a sudden, uplifting idea occurred, she simply waited until Lane left the company and, when everything was back to normal again, she then informed Kent. That way, his suspicions would be a thing of the past and it would not come as quite such a shock—well, she hoped not, anyway! And who knew, with both of them fighting him, perhaps Lane would decide it was not worth his while to continue opposing their divorce.

All she had to do was to hang on until Lane's departure, she decided happily once again, and with this reconciling thought to console her it was not long before she eventually fell asleep.

CHAPTER FOUR

IF she had thought Lane's absence meant she would
have an easy day on Monday, Jenna soon found that
was not going to be the case due to the amount of
telephone calls she was called upon to accept on his
behalf. In fact, it seemed by the end of the afternoon
that she had only managed to copy his report and
forward the required number to those concerned, and
very little else besides, except arrange future appoint-
ments and search out information for those callers
requiring it.

Thankfully though, her car had been returned as
promised and so her journey home was at least more
conveniently accomplished after work than it had
been in the morning, and after parking it at the rear
of her apartment building she made her way upstairs
quickly. Kent had arranged to take her out to dinner
that evening and she wanted to be ready when he
arrived.

On reaching the landing, however, she noticed a
young man wearing dark green overalls and carrying a
clipboard in his hand knocking on her door, and she
approached him with her brows drawing together
curiously as she wondered why he was calling at her
particular apartment. Evidently he must have seen her
too from the corner of his eye because he turned
towards her even before she arrived at her door, his
brows lifting enquiringly.

'Miss Bowman?' he hazarded.

'Yes,' she nodded, her interest becoming even more aroused.

'I'm from International Motors,' he advised, unconsciously endorsing the caption she could now see written on his front pocket. 'I've a car for you outside if you'd just like to sign this receipt.' He indicated a pink duplicate attached to his clipboard.

Jenna could not have appeared more stunned if she had tried. 'I'm sorry, but there must be some mistake,' she half laughed, shaking her head in confusion. 'I haven't had any dealings with International Motors.'

'No, that's all been taken care of. You only have to sign for it,' he explained, although not so it really made the matter any clearer for his listener. 'Oh, and there's this letter to go with it.' Extracting a plain white envelope from his board, he handed it to her.

Opening it quickly, Jenna's eyes understandably raced to the bottom of the page first, their dusky frames widening as Lane's authoritatively scrawled name leapt into view, then frowning again she raised her gaze in order to read the short note penned above. There was no salutation she discovered. It merely announced peremptorily,

'I dislike the idea of my wife, whether she calls herself Miss Bowman or not, taking unnecessary chances with her life. Therefore, in future kindly drive the vehicle delivered with this message and dispose of that other contraption!'

The tone as much as the content of the note had Jenna's temperature immediately rising, but nowhere near as much as it did when she chanced to look up and, before he could disguise it, caught a somewhat smirking expression on the face of the man before her.

He thought . . .! Oh, she knew exactly what he was thinking! She fumed as the heat of embarrassment washed over her. And how dared Lane put her in such a humiliating position! All because his ego would not let him accept the fact that he no longer had any rights where she was concerned! With deliberate movements she re-folded the page crisply, replaced it in the envelope, and handed it back to the overall-clad young man.

'As I said, there's been a mistake,' she bit out tautly.

It was his turn to frown now. 'But you are Miss Jenna Bowman, aren't you? And this is apartment No. 5, 109 Immarna Road?'

'Yes, you have the name and address correct . . . just the person wrong,' she replied, no doubt perplexingly to him, but with a definite meaning for herself. 'And I'm sorry you've been put to the trouble of delivering it for nothing, but it's not mine, and so I'd be pleased if you would return it to where it came from.'

'But—but . . .' He scratched at his head bewilderedly.

Jenna began inserting her key in the lock, her lips curving wryly. 'You may as well because I don't intend to sign for it.'

'Okay,' he gave in with a sigh. 'But the boss is sure going to have something to say when he hears about this.'

'As I'm sure mine will too,' she quipped drily, although more to herself than to him, as she slipped through the doorway. Though not before she had imparted some rather explicit words herself! followed the prompt and fervent avowal.

Jenna's thoughts continued in much the same fashion throughout the evening, leading Kent to remark aggrievedly, again, that she was too pre-occupied to even listen to a word he had to say, but as it was not a subject she could discuss with him—no matter how much she would have appreciated the release of being able to discuss it with *someone*—she could only plead a tiring weekend as her excuse, which he grudgingly accepted.

The following day she was no less deeply immersed in thought, though, as she waited impatiently for Lane to put in an appearance. Every time someone entered the main office she was the first to check to see who it was, and each time heaved a disgruntled sigh when it did not herald the man she was all too anxious to see. When it reached time to leave at the end of the day, she was reluctantly forced into conceding that she was just going to have to keep her annoyance for the morrow when Lane would undoubtedly return. Provided, of course, he had not altered his schedule once again without bothering to inform her!

Arriving at her apartment, Jenna promptly changed into a pair of shorts and a brief top, and poured herself a cold drink. It had been another boiling day, and her drive home into the lowering sun had not done anything to lessen the heat. The ensuing knock at her door had her responding casually, surmising it to be Kent. He had said he might drop by if his afternoon round of client calls brought him out her way. But to her surprise it was not Kent, it was Lane she abruptly found herself facing on opening the door, and who arrogantly entered without waiting to be invited.

Since she did not appear to have much choice, she closed the door decisively and swung round to stand with her hands resting on slender hips, her indignation at his high-handedness almost palpable.

'You wished to see me, I presume!' she stated caustically rather than questioned.

Lane's mouth firmed, his ebony lashed eyes sweeping over her savagely. 'I also thought that in five years you may have grown up to some extent!' he castigated. 'Just what did you think you were proving by returning that car?'

So that was what was biting him, was it? Well, she had something to say on that matter too! 'I would have thought that was obvious! I was proving I didn't intend to accept it!' she lashed back. 'But just for the record, what did *you* think you were proving by sending it in the first place?'

'I too would have thought that was quite evident!' His voice dripped with sarcasm. 'That I considered it necessary, if only to protect you from your own stupidity in persisting in driving an obviously broken-down vehicle!'

'It wasn't your decision to make!'

'Well, I did, and as far as I'm concerned that's the way it's going to remain!'

'Then you'd better just think again, because I won't be stood over by you or anyone else, and I shall continue to refuse to sign for it!'

'You don't have to any more! I've already done it for you! All I want from you are the keys to the Volkswagen in return for these.' He tossed a new set on to her dining table and began looking about him searchingly.

Guessing his intent, Jenna sprang to retrieve her bag from the bench in the adjoining kitchenette, but she was no match for either Lane's reflexes or strength as he wrested it from her effortlessly. Promptly turning it upside down in one furious movement, he spilled the contents over the bench, and once again beat her in their simultaneous grab for her keys, which he immediately pocketed in his pants.

'Give them back, Lane! You've no right to commandeer them like that!' she stormed wrathfully, but without really much hope of having him comply with her order. 'In any event, the car's still registered in my name, so there's nothing you can do with it. I—I'll report it as being stolen if you do take it!' Her threat was not altogether idly made.

'Then you can sign the release on the registration paper! Where is it, in here?' He picked up her wallet this time and started to open it.

'Don't you dare!' She made an infuriated, but vain attempt to snatch it away from him. 'I—I've got personal papers in there!'

Lane took not the slightest bit of notice but continued rifling through the contents until he located the paper he was seeking. Extracting it, he thumped it down on to the counter along with a pen that had previously rolled out of her bag.

'Sign it, Jenna!' he instructed in a forceful tone.

'No! And you can't make me either!'

'Can't I?' His lips twisted sardonically. 'I suggest you think some more about that.'

He was threatening her with Kent again, she smouldered, and her grey eyes shimmered brightly with unshed tears of impotent rage as they glared upwards. 'You really are an unscrupulous louse, aren't you, Lane? You don't hesitate to use our marriage as a lever whenever it's to your advantage, do you?'

'Why not? It seems to serve the purpose,' he shrugged indifferently. 'So why don't you just sign, and forget the self-pity bit, hmm? I would have thought you'd be grateful . . .'

'Grateful!' she cut in to expostulate. 'For what? Being forced to accept a car I neither asked for, nor want? Or for being put in the mortifying position of having to suffer the sniggering look on the face of the chap who delivered it because he assumed it was a gift for services I'd rendered as your—as your . . .' Just recalling the circumstances was sufficient to have her flushing warmly again.

'Mistress?' he supplied in a wryly humorous drawl. His brows peaked mockingly. 'Another reason you shouldn't have reverted to your maiden name, perhaps?'

Jenna's breasts heaved beneath her flimsy top. Having succeeded in enforcing his will on her yet one more time, she supposed bitterly that he could permit himself to relax and find something at her expense to amuse him!

'And I meant, grateful—not for the car, but for the fact that I haven't yet disclosed our relationship to Sharman,' Lane took the opportunity to relay.

'Why would you?' she half laughed acidly. 'As you said, it's serving its purpose only too well!'

'Except that you still haven't signed over the registration,' he reminded drily.

Knowing further resistance was futile, she finally, irately, scribbled her signature on the appropriate line. 'There! Now would you mind giving me back my wallet?' she demanded on a tart note. He still had it in his hand and was presently engaged in glancing leisurely at the photos it contained.

When he made no move to heed her, Jenna tried taking it from him by force again, only to have it rapidly removed from her reach as Lane continued to study one particular print. A glimpse was enough to inform her that it was one that had been taken on their honeymoon and, not for the first time, she began calling herself all manner of fools for having retained it.

'I meant to throw that out years ago,' she now asserted with a deprecating hunching of her honey toned shoulders.

'Pity . . . it's a good likeness of you.' With his head tilting slightly he suddenly swung his gaze in her direction in order to scrutinise her with the same intentness, and which she found infinitely more disturbing. 'You don't look to have altered much either. I wonder if you have in other ways,' he mused, and before she knew what was happening, a hand had snaked out to tangle within her hair and propel her closer to his muscular frame as his mouth lowered to take possession of hers purposefully.

Temporarily, Jenna was too startled to even think of resisting, but as the pressure of his lips became more demanding her seemingly frozen senses abruptly blazed with life once more. Now a haphazard mass of feelings engulfed her. Fury, indignation, chagrin, and . . . oh God, no, not pleasure! she despaired as she felt herself impulsively beginning to respond.

Lifting his head briefly, Lane surveyed her somewhat bemused features with lazy eyes. 'Hmm . . . you always did have the most delightfully tantalising mouth,' he murmured ruefully, and promptly renewed his devastating attack on her lips, and floundering emotions.

Without time to recover, it was an onslaught she was as equally unable to withstand as she had the first,

Jenna discovered to her dismay as her lips immediately parted beneath the compelling touch of his, and fervently clung in a way they never had with Kent. A shocking realisation that had her catching at her lower lip with shining white teeth and backing away agitatedly when he eventually released her.

Lane merely seemed amused by her shaken reaction and calmly exchanged her wallet for the registration paper which he folded and inserted in his shirt pocket. 'You never used to look so stricken when I kissed you,' he bantered, his lips twisting crookedly, as he passed her on his way to the door. Reaching it, he turned to cast her a measuring glance for a moment, his expression firming again. 'Just make certain you use that car, though, hmm? Because I'll be watching to see that you do.' And with an accentuating nod he left the apartment as self-assuredly as he had entered it.

His departure had Jenna emerging from her seeming trance abruptly as a sudden remembrance occurred and rushing after him. He was half way down the stairs by then and she called to him urgently from the landing. 'Lane! My keys for the apartment are on that ring too!'

Halting, he fished the bunch out of his pocket and held them up. 'Which ones?'

Jenna moved down the stairs until their heads were almost level. 'Those are the only two for the VW,' she pointed out resignedly and waited while he removed them before returning the rest to her. 'And—umm— just as a matter of interest,' she added a little self-consciously, 'where do I find this car, and—and what make is it?' If the keys on her table did not have the manufacturer's name on them, it could be extremely embarrassing, not to say apparently suspicious, having to try them on every likely vehicle outside the building in order to find the one they fitted!

'You didn't even bother to ask yesterday?' He shook his head in a mixture of wry amusement and disbelief.

'Since I wasn't planning on accepting it, there didn't seem much point,' she grimaced.

He sighed, but whether in vexation or tedium she could not tell. 'It's out the front, and it's an Alpha Romeo.' Followed by a raising of his well defined brows to an ironic peak. 'Would I expect my wife to drive anything less than I do?' He continued down the stairs with a loose-limbed tread without waiting for a reply.

For a time Jenna would not have been in a position to give him one even if he had waited, so great was her surprise. She had anticipated the car being something far more ordinary—in keeping with her certainly less than affluent lifestyle—and the fact that it was not had her returning to the apartment with creases of suspicion starting to mark her forehead.

It was not that she knew he could not be generous to a fault at times, but in view of the circumstances existing between them at present, she could not quite bring herself to believe that generosity had been his sole motive. If it had been a less conspicuous make she would have been able to claim she had just decided to update on the spur of the moment and was paying it off, but as secretaries at her level did not usually splash out on such imported vehicles, it would be an almost impossible allegation to make sound feasible ... the more so where Kent was concerned! And exactly as Lane indisputably knew as well! she fumed lividly. Storming through to the kitchenette, she began returning all the spilled articles to her bag in furious movements. Oh, she could slay him for this! she railed. That was, the discomposing thought promptly followed, if Kent did not do the same to her first!

As appeared more than likely the following morning when he arrived at the office in time to see Jenna alighting from the pale blue Alpha as he drove into the yard—of all days for him to have put in an appearance at the plant prior to commencing his morning rounds!—and determinedly cornered her in the staff tea room adjoining the main office as soon as possible.

'Who the hell's car is that you're driving?' was his initial, heavily frowned demand.

Jenna took a deep breath but continued pouring herself a cup of coffee. 'M-mine.' She had not been able to think of anyone else she could even say had lent it to her.

'Since when?'

'Y-yesterday.' The hand spooning sugar into her mug as unsteady as her voice now.

'Oh?' His blue eyes narrowed intently. 'And how would you come by a vehicle like that?'

'How does anyone come by one?' she countered, making an effort to shrug nonchalantly. 'I bought it, naturally.'

'Don't give me that!' he discounted harshly. 'You hardly had enough funds to fix the Volkswagen the last time it needed attention. You sure didn't have sufficient to buy a ruddy Alpha, of all things!'

'But that's just it,' she said swiftly. 'I *couldn't* keep affording to repair it all the time, so when it started playing up again last Sunday, I—I decided to get rid of it.'

'So you could replace it with an Alpha Romeo?' he guffawed with jeering incredulity. Quietening again, his gaze settled on her sourly. 'But that's right, you did say Forrester drove you home Sunday evening, didn't you? In fact, you're spending more and more time in his company these days, nor have you been the same person since you started working for him! And that's where your new car came from, isn't it, Jenna? *Isn't it?*' He shook her roughly, infuriatedly, by the shoulders.

'No!' she denied frantically. 'I told you . . . I bought it!'

'With money you just happened to find laying around, I suppose!'

She lifted her chin in an attempt at defiance. 'No, on—on time payment, as it so happens.'

'Oh, yeah?' His lip curled derisively. 'You may have got it for payment all right, but I bet it sure as hell wasn't on time!'

'How dare you!' Jenna wrenched out of his grasp and sent a successfully swinging hand to crack forcefully across his cheek. That his thoughts should have so openly coincided with those of the man who had originally delivered the car was just too much! 'I thought you knew me better than to make such an offensive insinuation as that, Kent!' she censured hotly.

With the imprint of her hand still visibly red against his skin, he faced her tautly, his breathing deep. 'Well, where did you get the money for it, then?' he rasped, though in a somewhat more diffident manner.

'I told you . . . I got a loan!'

'Just so you could buy the same make of car as Forrester's?' The corners of his mouth turned down sceptically. 'You think I don't know he also drives one of those?'

'So?' She widened her eyes sardonically. 'There's a lot of others who do too, or are you now suggesting that Lane provided them with theirs as well?'

'No, of course not.' He shook his head irritably. 'But why so suddenly, and why an Alpha, for God's sake?'

She executed a deprecating shrug. 'Why not? I like them, and it's not as if it's one of their most expensive models.' That, she had been relieved to discover! 'Besides, the offer I was made was impossible to refuse.' A truth, if ever there was one!

'You'll still be paying it off for years!'

'Probably,' she didn't mind conceding. But at least it wasn't going to cost as much as Lane had intended, she noted with considerable satisfaction, for although it had been touch and go there for a while, Kent did appear to be calming down a little now.

'And after we're married?' he enquired flatly.

Surmising it was not a judicious time to remind him she had not yet said she would marry him—her contentions to Lane notwithstanding—Jenna smiled whimsically. 'We could always sell it, I guess.' It appealed to her sense of humour to imagine her ex-husband, as he would be by then, providing them with such a wedding present.

Kent expelled an eloquent breath, reaching for her again, but gently this time and holding her close. 'I only wish it was soon,' he groaned. 'I'm sure I only get these fits of jealousy because you're not mine the way I want you to be. And I *do* want you so very, very much, Jen!' With his hands cupping her face he tilted her head upwards so he could claim her lips hungrily.

Suddenly there came the sound of a throat being cleared, expressively, and as Jenna pulled away, embarrassed, she caught sight of Lane standing in the doorway, his eyes glittering fiercely, his mouth thinning to an uncompromising line.

'I think you'd better consider yourself fired, Sharman!' he ground out coldly. 'I'm not having your amorous interludes conducted in my offices, and since you obviously find it impossible to leave my secretary alone . . . Come and see me in an hour's time and I'll have your wages and papers ready for you!' He sent Jenna one last unsparing glare that slashed over her derogatorily before turning on his heel and striding for his office.

'He's got to be kidding!' Kent ejaculated, a stunned look on his face. 'I was only kissing you, and it wasn't as if we were in full view of everyone!'

Just in the wrong person's view! qualified Jenna silently, as anger began overcoming her own shock. She was willing to lay odds Lane had been sweating on just such an opportunity to exact a little more of his revenge, but she considered it most unfair that Kent should be made to pay also.

'Yes—well—I'll go and speak to him,' she offered stiltedly.

'Not on my account, thanks!' he refused categorically. 'If there's any talking to be done, I'll do it myself! Although if he's that intolerant I think I'd rather work elsewhere anyway.'

Interrupted by the phone on her desk ringing, she gave him a consoling half smile and hurried to answer it. Her suspicions regarding the caller's identity proven correct when Lane immediately ordered her into his office.

'I'm not surprised Hodgson Industries was in such dire straits if that's how you've all been occupying your time!' he denounced blisteringly the minute the door was shut behind her. 'Don't you have anything more important to do than spend the morning kissing all the men in the office?'

Jenna's hands clenched angrily, but guessing she was not going to do Kent's cause any good by losing her temper, she made every effort to hang on to it. 'It wasn't *all* of them, just one,' she modified tightly. 'And you're not being fair to Kent, dismissing him over something so trivial.'

'*Trivial!*' he echoed on an abrasive note. 'You call it trivial for me to find another man kissing my wife under my very nose, and in one of my own offices, at that!'

'And as you're very well aware, Kent doesn't know we're married!'

'But you do, don't you, *my love*?'

Since she could hardly refute it, she exchanged defence for attack. 'Not that I recall that appearing to cause you much concern when the languid Miss Cornell came visiting! Or was that just your mouth-to-mouth resucitation technique you were practising?' she retorted in a tone laced with sarcasm.

'And as you may also recollect, that until you came blundering in, we also had the door shut!'

That was supposed to make it acceptable? 'So next time we'll close the door!' she snapped.

Lane smiled, humourlessly, and shook his head. 'Except that for you and Sharman there won't *be* a next time!' he declared, stonily dogmatic.

Jenna combed her fingers through her gold-streaked hair distractedly and tried to re-gather her thoughts.

'And you're still doing Kent an injustice by using such a feeble excuse to sack him,' she maintained steadfastly. Particularly when she surmised it was only a way for him to get back at her. 'It's not something that's ever happened before, and—and . . .'

'So why start now?' he interrupted, his eyes ranging over her relentlessly.

The unwavering appraisal made her nervous and as a result had her revealing what she would rather have kept private. 'I—we—we'd just had a—er—slight altercation.'

'About what?'

As if he could not guess! 'The car you forced me to accept!' Her grey eyes darkened with resentment.

'Oh?' A satirical curve caught at the edges of his sensuous mouth. 'And what's that got to do with him?'

Jenna stiffened at the pseudo-innocent question but clamped down on her rising emotions determinedly. 'Well, naturally he wanted to know where it had come from. He knows I'd be struggling to afford it on my salary.'

'Is that a subtle way of asking for an increase in your wages?' The mockery in his voice was quite evident now.

'No!' she was just able to get out tersely between rigid lips.

'So what was the conclusion he came to regarding the source of the donation?'

Her chin angled protectively higher. 'I—I told him I bought it on hire-purchase.'

'A claim I gather he didn't accept since you argued about it,' Lane made his own shrewd deduction, his ensuing laugh unattractive. 'He doesn't trust you much, does he, Jenna? But then, maybe he has reason not to.'

On her own behalf Jenna was not prepared to be quite so reticent and her eyes sparkled with an irate light. 'That's a contemptible thing to imply, Lane!' she condemned. 'As well as being totally without foundation!'

'Sharman apparently doesn't think so,' he shrugged unremorsefully.

'Why wouldn't he while you're doing your best to ensure he does!' She sucked in a calming breath, her expression bitter. 'You've changed, Lane. You never used to be so scheming and—and vengeful.'

He flexed both shoulders in a gesture of complete unconcern. 'A great many things have changed during the last five years, though, haven't they, my pet? Including you!' The last was bitten out piercingly.

Ignoring the strange feeling of dejection the comment engendered, Jenna pressed on tenaciously. 'That's still no reason to take it out on Kent. He's one of our best reps and surely deserves another chance.' She paused, gathering courage and forcibly suppressing her pride. 'Won't you please reconsider?'

'No!' His refusal was flat and unconditional. 'I told you—I've no intention of putting up with him kissing my wife in front of me at every opportunity.'

'And as I said, it's not at every opportunity, it was just once!' Jenna fired back losing control. 'And stop referring to me as your wife! You know as well as I do that I haven't been that for some time now.'

Lane fixed her with a coolly calculating stare. 'Then perhaps that should be remedied,' he asserted sharply.

If his expression had been different, Jenna would

have believed he was joking, but as it was she returned his gaze uneasily. Just what nefarious plan was he hatching in that fertile brain of his now? However, she did at least manage to project a little confidence in her wryly half-laughed reply.

'Something I'm sure definitely wouldn't suit either of us. Especially in view of the fact that I'm planning to marry Kent.'

'In that regard you're forgetting one small thing, though, aren't you?' His brows rose to goading heights. 'You aren't free to marry him, but you *are* still married to me ... and will remain so for some time to come.'

'Because you're too gutless to become involved with the over-indulged Rosalind Cornell without the safety of a wife somewhere in the background to protect you in case she becomes a complication!' she charged, sarcastically scornful.

'Uh-uh,' he disclaimed with an unexpected indolence. 'Rosalind's not likely to become a complication. Just the opposite, actually.'

'In which case, you have no grounds for trying to stop my association with Kent continuing!'

Lane waved a dissenting finger. 'Not stopping it from continuing ... just from developing to its fullest extent,' he amended in a mocking drawl. 'Plus refusing to have the affair conducted in my offices, of course.'

'We weren't, and you know it!' indignation had her blazing back swiftly. Then, after an effort, in a more moderate tone, 'And I still say you're being unreasonable in taking it out on Kent. Won't you please think it over?'

'Pleading for the man you love, Jenna?' he gibed

sneeringly. 'Did he think he'd stand a better chance if you did his begging for him?'

'No, he did not!' she was pleased to be able to repudiate. 'As a matter of fact, he didn't want me to speak to you about it at all! His reaction being, that if you were that narrow-minded he would rather leave anyway!'

Lane studied her slightly flushed features speculatively and then his lips shaped sardonically. 'You may rest your case now, Miss Bowman. Just send Sharman in, will you? I may as well see him now as later.'

Jenna sighed, partly turning towards the door and then swinging back again. 'H-have you decided to give him a second chance, Lane?' she could not restrain herself from probing, even if tentatively. His tone had not been exactly encouraging.

And nor was the savage glance she received in return for her query, she noted despondently, as he rebuffed inflexibly. 'That, Miss Bowman, is my decision, and none of your business!'

Kent was waiting outside when she emerged, and entered the office immediately she relayed that Lane wanted to see him. Apart from an indecisive shrug there was not time for her to give him a hint as to what his reception might be, although she knew what she was disconsolately expecting, and after pouring herself a fresh mug of coffee she returned to her desk to await the inevitable outcome.

Half an hour later Kent was still closeted with her husband, and Jenna's anxieties began to increase. Lane could not possibly be so ruthless as to not only dismiss Kent but also, as a parting gift, divulge their relationship to him too, could he? she wondered apprehensively. Not that she would not have preferred Kent to know now, of course, but if Lane did take it into his head to do so she did not doubt his method of revelation would be mercilessly designed to create an impassable chasm between Kent and herself. And if that was not the reason their encounter was taking so long, then what on earth was?

When Kent did finally reappear he walked over to Jenna's desk with such a contemplative look on his face that she could not decide just what had occurred, as evidenced by her worried enquiry, 'Well, are you still on the payroll or not?'

'Mmm, although not here. In fact, would you believe . . . I've been promoted?' he half laughed in a somewhat bemused manner.

'To what?' she frowned, more than a little perplexed herself by now.

'Sales Manager—with one of the company's other subsidiaries,' he disclosed in the same abstracted fashion. 'You know, I always said I thought I'd like working under our new management, and he's,' with an explicit nod over his shoulder, 'a real good bloke once you get to know him . . . as well as on the ball!' in obvious admiration. 'Once I'd recovered from the discovery that I wasn't going to be fired after all, we had quite a talk and he gave me a number of pointers about the business that should really stand me in good stead when I've got my own team working for me in Brisbane.'

'Did you say *Brisbane*?' Jenna promptly sought verification in a seething undertone.

'That's right,' he smiled enthusiastically, and with patent satisfaction. 'Apparently there's a vacancy for a Sales Manager up there and the boss thinks I've got just the right qualifications to take on the position. He said he'd been quite impressed with my sales figures for some time now.'

Jenna could have screamed with rage and frustration. So yet again Lane had scored another success against her. As he obviously took exception to her relationship with Kent, what better way to thwart it than by removing one half of it to an entirely different state! Particularly when that half appeared more than happy to go along with the idea! she smouldered. Not that she altogether blamed Kent. As Freda had observed that first day, Lane could be a real charmer when it suited him, and rather than lose one of their best salesmen completely, it had evidently been expedient for him to assume such a role on this occasion.

'You're in favour of the arrangement, then, I gather?' she could not help grimacing.

'Very much so, naturally,' he nodded vigorously. 'Why wouldn't I be? It's a great opportunity for me to make something of myself within the company, and . . .' he hesitated, smiling persuasively, 'I thought for us to get married. The idea of being parted from you is the only point against it as far as I can see. So how about it, hmm? We could be married on Saturday in time to leave on the Monday. And I'm sure you'll like living in Queensland.'

Among all his comments—most of which she nervously shied away from—one stood out glaringly for Jenna. 'You're leaving on Monday?' she gasped. That was less than a week away! Lane obviously had not intended to allow any grass to grow under his feet, or Kent's! she noted vexedly.

'Mmm, that's right,' he verified. 'But more importantly, what about the other, Jen? Will you marry me and come with me?' A pleading note entered his voice. 'You must know how much I want you to.'

Jenna gnawed at her lip discomfitedly, all the while railing at her husband for having landed her in such a predicament. 'Yes—well—I'd like to, I really would, but it—it's such short notice,' she parried. 'Even without the lease on the apartment, it would be almost impossible for me to make all the necessary arrangements for leaving in such a few days, and—and if you're expected to take over this position immediately don't you think it would be less of a hassle if you were able to give all your attention to settling in with the job if you didn't also have the added worry of finding somewhere suitable for us to live? I mean, it's all right living in an apartment when you're single, but surely you'd want a house once you're married, and finding the right one can be time-consuming, you know.'

'But you could do all that while I was at work during the day.'

'Maybe, but there would still be times when a decision by you would be required, as well as—as furniture to choose, which is really something that should be done together, and you would need *some* time to relax, especially with all the extra work entailed in taking over a new position. If you hope to do it successfully, that is.'

'So what are you suggesting? That you stay here, while I go north on my own?' he queried on a disappointed and rather disgruntled note.

She spread her hands helplessly wide. 'Well, I really think that's the most sensible solution, even if it's not the most attractive. At least until you've had a chance to become conversant with the work.' A hopefully inspired thought presented itself. 'It would be such a pity if you were demoted again because your performance wasn't up to scratch due to your having too many extraneous matters on your mind.'

'Mmm, I hadn't thought of that,' Kent conceded meditatively. 'And if I fail at this I may not be given another opportunity.'

Jenna seized upon his dubiousness with alacrity. 'Quite possibly, I should say, in view of the number of powerhouse employees that were present at the conference last weekend. Forrester's don't seem to lack for eager beavers. While in the meantime,' she hurried on encouragingly, 'we can always keep in touch by post or phone, and maybe I could even fly up to Brisbane for the weekend occasionally. Or you fly down here, if it comes to that.'

'Hmm . . .? The latter probably wouldn't be much trouble, but . . .' his lips curved obliquely, 'you wouldn't be able to afford the fare while you're paying that car off, would you?'

'Oh, I expect I'd be able to manage somehow,' she claimed lightly. 'If you'd really like me to visit you, of course.'

'God, you don't know!' Kent exclaimed, taking an impassioned step towards her, then on remembering where he was bringing himself up short. 'It's going to be purgatory being unable to see you whenever I want.'

'Although you do agree my idea of waiting a while is more practical?'

'I guess so,' he sighed reluctantly. 'As much as it goes against the grain to admit it.'

From Jenna's standpoint his concurrence was an alleviating reprieve, although it was becoming increasingly apparent that the time was swiftly approaching when she would be unable to keep her secret from him any longer. All she could continue hoping for, was that Lane had returned to head office before that time eventually arrived.

As soon as Kent took his departure, though, Jenna made a beeline for her husband's room again, and on this occasion she was the one to burst into censuring speech immediately she was inside.

'I suppose you consider it quite amusing shipping Kent off to Queensland!' she blazed.

'Not at all,' Lane denied blandly, shrugging. 'But then, I didn't find anything humorous in having my offices turned into some sort of lovers' rendezvous either.' And without giving her time to object to the exaggeration, continued in a hardening tone, 'Nonetheless, just for your information, I've always made it a policy of my companies, the same as many others do, not to have wives or girl-friends working in the same office as their husbands or boyfriends ... and Sharman is no exception!'

She may have been persuaded to accept the idea, except for one thing. 'Then how come you haven't displayed the same objections to *our* working together? Or doesn't that contravene your supposed regulations?' she sniped.

His duskily outlined hazel-green eyes held hers sardonically. 'How could it when I have it on the best authority, namely you, that you haven't been my wife for some time now? Moreover, you do call yourself *Miss* Bowman, don't you, my love?'

He had an answer for everything! she fumed, but still could not stop herself from gibing, 'So when did this vacancy occur in Brisbane? The minute you came to the conclusion that would be an even more effective manner of parting Kent and me than by sacking him?'

A dark brow quirked upwards. 'Sharman certainly didn't appear averse to going,' he countered rather than answered.

'In view of the trumped-up story you fed him, I'm not surprised!'

'Uh-uh!' He shook his head lazily. 'As you should know, my pet, business is strictly business where I'm concerned, and because he *is* one of our best reps, as you so correctly pointed out, I've been toying with the idea of sending him north for almost a week now.'

'The same as you were considering firing him?' she scoffed tartly, not altogether believing.

'Oh, but he is dismissed . . . at least from this company for the time being,' Lane drawled, his eyes mocking. 'Besides, he needed pulling into line, if only to remind him to keep his mind on the work he's being paid to do.'

Jenna grimaced, expelling a defeated sigh. It was not that she was convinced—deep down some instinct still told her that her association with Kent had some bearing on his decision—it was just all too evident there was no way she could force him into admitting as much.

'Well, even if we do have to endure a temporary separation, we still intend to marry,' she maintained defiantly as she made for the door.

'Mmm, so he said.'

Coming to a shocked halt, she whirled to face him again. 'Kent told *you* we planned to marry?' Her eyes registered her incredulity.

'Uh-huh!' he confirmed indolently, his mouth curving with patent amusement. 'He apparently thought it only fair to warn me that he intended marrying my secretary and taking her with him. Naturally I said that was wholly your decision to make.' He paused, his smile widening tauntingly. 'So tell me, just what was your reply, my love? Are you intending to enter a bigamous marriage? I'd be interested to hear, believe me.'

'Oh, go to hell, Lane! Just go to hell!' she hurled at him, incensed and exasperated, as she slammed out of the room. He would be waiting until doomsday before she added to his amusement by endorsing what he already must have known!

CHAPTER FIVE

IN the weeks that followed Jenna's workload remained as high as it had ever been, but although she appreciated the extra money the overtime provided, the amount of hours she was putting in was still quite wearing. How Lane could keep up the pace without showing any signs of fatigue, she did not know, but she supposed the fact that the company was beginning to show satisfying results in return for his efforts may have accounted for it. He certainly had the Midas touch, she conceded, because Hodgson's were experiencing an unprecedented growth in production and sales were soaring.

Kent continued to keep in contact, by letter and phone only, though, so far—and was apparently thoroughly enjoying both his promotion and his transfer to the Sunshine State—but without his company Jenna found time starting to hang heavily on her hands when she did manage a night or two away from work, and after he had been gone about a month she decided to visit her parents the following weekend. She had not seen them since her holidays and she thought a break from the city might help to revive her slightly wilted spirits.

The only flaw in the arrangement that she could see would be her mother, she mused wryly. For although both her parents had been wonderfully supportive after her break-up with Lane, even if a shade disappointed and disapproving, she was all too conscious just what her mother's reaction would be when she discovered the source of her daughter's newly acquired vehicle. There would be no point attempting to spin them the same story she had Kent. They knew her, and her casual philosophy regarding her means of transport, far too well for Jenna to even remotely believe they would be taken in by such an explanation. Despite all that had occurred, there was still no one quite like Lane in her mother's eyes, and unquestionably his providing her with a new car would only serve to strengthen the conviction. Why, even when she had taken Kent to meet her parents, it had been a case of, 'He seems very pleasant, but not as nice as Lane, though, dear,' from her mother, she recalled. Still, it would be a nice change to get away for a couple of days, she resolved, and if her and her mother's opinions did not agree concerning her husband, well, at least they had never allowed it to spoil their own close relationship.

As it happened, however, Jenna did not get to visit her parents that weekend anyway, because after having been away from the office for the preceding three days conducting some business on the south coast, Lane phoned her at home shortly after dinner on the Friday night.

'I'm sorry, but I'd like you to come out to the house tonight and take some dictation for me,' he did not beat about the bush but came straight to the point. 'I couldn't get back to the office in time to give it to you this afternoon, and as you know I'm due to leave again for Brisbane on Sunday evening.' One arrangement she had been informed about! 'Not only are there some letters and memos I want to get off as soon as possible, but there's a sheaf of notes to be coordinated, as well as instructions for what I want done while I'm absent.' He paused. 'Oh, and you'd better bring a bag with you, you'll be staying overnight.'

'What for?' she was surprised into questioning.

'In case we don't get through it all tonight. Or I happen to remember something else in the morning when I'll hopefully have a little less on my mind,' came the drily sardonic retort.

Jenna pulled a disgruntled face at the phone. Why did he always have to choose a weekend when she had something planned? Was he psychic? 'I *was* going away for the weekend,' she complained. She doubted it would alter the outcome but felt she was entitled to lodge some sort of protest all the same.

'Again! Who with this time?'

'I wasn't going *with* anyone!' she emphasised testily, provoked by the caustic intonation in his voice. 'I'd arranged to drive up to Mum and Dad's, as a matter of fact.'

'Then you'd better give them my apologies when you let them know you won't be going,' he directed, and because she knew, in that regard at least, that he was sincere, she unconsciously nodded. 'How are they, anyway?'

Still singing your praises! she quipped peevishly to herself. Aloud: 'Oh, fine. Or at least they were at the thought of seeing me for the weekend.' She could not resist the pointed addition.

Lane laughed. A warm resonant sound that brought a lump to her throat as it abruptly conjured up sweet memories. 'Sorry, my love, but it can't be helped.'

She swallowed heavily. 'Yes, well, what time do you want me over there?'

'How soon can you make it?' There was still a trace

of laughter in his tone and it had her throat constricting anew.

'I—umm—I'm not sure,' she stammered thickly. 'I'll have to ring Mum and let her know, of course, and—and . . .' Faltering to a stop, she made a concentrated effort to pull herself together, and forced out with feigned humour, 'I guess what I'm trying to say is, I'll be there as soon as I can make it.'

There was a moment's silence on the line and then she could almost visualise him frowning as he probed acutely, 'Is anything wrong?'

Oh, yes, there was something wrong all right when you suddenly discovered the husband from whom you had been separated for five years still had the power to disturb your composure in such a fashion as he just had hers! she allowed ruefully. For his edification, though, it was another matter now that she thankfully had her feelings tightly under control once more.

'Apart from having another of my weekends commandeered, you mean?' she countered, adequately pert.

'Hmm . . . I should have known better than to have asked,' he drawled wryly. 'Okay, I'll see you when you get here.'

Jenna's following call to her mother took longer than she expected. Due mainly to the fact that she felt obliged to pass on Lane's apologies as he had suggested, and which immediately had her parent asking a welter of questions because until then Jenna had conveniently concealed the fact from her that she and Lane had even come across each other again, let alone that she was actually working for him. Eventually, however, even her mother's queries ran out and she was at last able to replace the receiver.

With her overnight bag already packed, it only took a few minutes to lock the apartment and then she was hurrying down the stairs. She was later than she had anticipated already, and did not doubt Lane would accuse her of deliberately being so.

Which accounted for her first words when she finally arrived. 'I'm sorry I took so long but Mum wouldn't—er—let me off the phone,' she part apologised, part explained. Halting momentarily, she then relayed grudgingly, 'She and Dad both send their regards.'

Lane dipped his head in acknowledgment. 'That was kind of them. I hope you also remembered to pass on my apologies for depriving them of your company.' He slanted her an enquiring glance as he led the way into the office.

'Of course,' Jenna nodded. Her lips twitched wryly. 'That's why it took me so long on the phone with Mum. They hadn't realised we'd met again.'

Depositing her bag by the door with the comment, 'I'll get Floyd to take that up for you shortly,' he eyed her askance. 'You've been keeping it a secret from them?'

'Not really,' she shrugged discomfitedly, and moving restlessly beneath his astute gaze. Her head lifted fractionally higher. 'There didn't seem any reason to mention it, that's all.'

'No, naturally not,' he acceded, but so satirically that she coloured self-consciously and moved swiftly towards the desk.

'Yes, well, shall we get started?' she said in her most businesslike manner as she armed herself with pad and pencil.

For a time Lane continued to survey her intently,

then with a careless hunching of one shoulder he lowered his supple length into a studded leather chair and almost immediately began dictating. But at such a clipped and rapid rate that Jenna initially had trouble in keeping up with him. Nor as the evening wore on could she decide whether it was as a result of the amount of information he wished recorded, or whether he was just plain annoyed about something. Whatever the cause, though, it was certainly keeping her on her toes, the observation was ruefully made, and she was thankful for the opportunity to add a few more outlines to her notes to aid in their later translation when Mrs Squires' appearance with a tray of savouries and a pot of steaming coffee brought a short respite.

Forgoing the coffee, Lane adjourned to the conference room-cum-library adjoining to pour himself a stiff whisky instead, almost half of which he downed in his first mouthful. He *was* annoyed about something, deduced Jenna as she sipped thoughtfully at her own warm drink but just what about she could not fathom. Perhaps because he would rather have been enjoying Rosalind's flattering company instead of having to suffer hers, she mused, the thought automatically pulling her curving mouth pleasurably upwards. Since he had arbitrarily decided work should part her from Kent, why shouldn't she take satisfaction from the circumstances that prevented him from seeing his lady love?

The only other interruption during the remainder of the evening was by Floyd coming to take Jenna's bag upstairs, but it was still nearing midnight before they finally finished and, stretching, Lane leant back in his chair to resume his somewhat unnerving contemplation of her.

Avoiding his gaze, Jenna busily began gathering papers and folders into a neat pile, only then looking up to enquire diffidently, 'Do you want all this typed tomorrow?'

He shook his head briefly. 'No, at the office on Monday will do. You can sign them.'

'You're sure you can trust me not to make any mistakes?' she gibed half-heartedly. She wasn't too sure just what to make of his attitude at the moment, but his earlier unwarranted aspersions regarding her work still rankled.

'It would appear so, wouldn't it?' He gained his feet in a swift, lithe action and taking his glass with him headed for the library once more, returning with the crystal container refilled.

Not knowing quite what to do next, Jenna bent to lift the coffee tray his housekeeper had left with them. 'I'll just take this out to the kitchen,' she murmured.

'Don't bother!' he promptly vetoed. 'Enid will collect it in the morning.'

'Oh, but I don't mind, and . . .'

'That's a change!' he broke in, markedly sarcastic, and drained a fair portion of his drink. 'As I recall, you always used to complain because you *didn't* have a housekeeper to do everything for you!'

She made a deprecating movement with her hands. 'I—I never seemed to have the time to do it all myself.'

'That's right, you were too busy being the social butterfly, weren't you?' he stabbed at her scornfully.

'I thought that was what was expected of me . . . at first,' she defended in a small voice, knowing he was not altogether wrong. 'I'd never mixed in—in such circles before.'

His upper lip curled derogatorily above the rim of his glass. 'So you decided to outdo them instead!'

Looking back on it, she supposed that must have been how it appeared, although that really had not been her intention. 'No, I simply wanted some company,' she sighed. Then, in a more aggressive tone, 'And strange as it may seem, my husband's for preference!'

Lane took another mouthful of whisky. 'I was trying to ensure the business never went downhill again!'

'In that case, you got what *you* wanted, didn't you?' Jenna muttered bitterly.

'And now you think Sharman's going to do the same for you, is that it?' A bitingly mocking half laugh issued from his bronzed throat.

'At least he couldn't do worse!' she was stung into sniping.

'Provided he gets the opportunity!'

'*When* he gets the opportunity!' she corrected insistently, snatching up her shoulder bag from the desk. 'And since this conversation doesn't appear to be achieving anything, if you have no objections, I think I'll go to bed. It's late and I'm tired.' Her eyes met his aloofly. 'Do I have the same room as before?'

Lane inclined his dark head sardonically. 'I believe so.'

'Thank you,' she returned crisply. 'Then goodnight.' She spun on her heel and marched out of the office with her head held high.

Upstairs, Jenna located her lilac decorated bedroom without any difficulty, but after showering and donning a very brief, very sheer, apricot lace nightdress, suddenly found her brain too active for sleep. So instead of climbing into the comfortably wide bed, she turned out all the lights except for a small beside lamp and padded out on to the balcony. It was a lovely warm night with only enough of a sea-scented breeze to ruffle a few strands of her hair occasionally, and resting her forearms on the white-painted parapet, she allowed her thoughts to wander.

She was still at a loss to understand the reason for Lane's behaviour during the evening. It was almost as if he had been deliberately trying to provoke an argument, and yet that evidently had not been his mood when he had telephoned her. Although considering the effect he had managed to have on her on the phone, maybe his unaccountable change had been a blessing in disguise, she conceded ruefully. Tilting her head back, she breathed deeply of the clear, clean smelling air, her eyes closing as the soft breeze stroked her creamily smooth skin, and then flashing wide open again as she whirled on hearing a sound in the room behind her.

'Jenna?' Lane's half puzzled, half exasperated voice carried out to her. 'Where in hell are you?'

'I'm out here . . . on the balcony,' she disclosed reluctantly, but grateful at least for the deep shadows that helped camouflage the flimsiness of her attire. 'What do you want?'

'That's a leading question,' he drawled as he came to prop himself negligently against the door frame, his tone informing her more adequately than words that whatever had been bugging him earlier had now disappeared.

Of course, whether that was a good thing or not, she could not quite decide. Dressed in a mid-thigh length towelling robe that was belted loosely about his lean waist and which revealed a broad expanse of his tanned chest, he looked more overwhelmingly male than she cared to admit. His obviously damp hair hugged closely to his well-shaped head and she wondered inconsequentially if it had been his shower that had cleared his mind of his previous ill-humour.

'Well, why are you in my room?' she re-phrased her question with some asperity as she pressed herself protectively further back among the shadows.

His thickly lashed eyes roamed over her leisurely— to her embarrassment. 'That's such an—umm— fetching outfit you're nearly wearing, I've almost forgotten.'

'Then until you remember, I'd be pleased if you would just get out!' she hissed.

His mouth curved in aggravatingly unperturbed amusement. 'I only said I'd *almost* forgotten.' And shrugging, 'I just wanted to ask if I'd mentioned in those notes that I wanted to speak to Ian before that new run of resistors goes into production. I couldn't remember.'

'Perhaps if you'd drunk coffee instead of whisky you'd be able to!' she retorted with a definite snap.

He made a disapproving clicking sound with his tongue. 'Not nice, my love,' he grinned, unabashed. 'So did I, or didn't I?'

'It was the last one you dictated!' The information was conveyed in sardonicaly eloquent tones.

Lane gave a slow, contemplative nod, as if in jogged remembrance, but to Jenna's annoyance, and continued self-consciousness, made no move to depart. 'I'll be seeing Sharman on Monday, of course,' he unexpectedly remarked on a casual note.

'And?' She stiffened, eyeing him warily.

'Oh, for heaven's sake, stop huddling in the corner,

he directed in a wryly humorous drawl and, catching her offguard, grasped her wrist with inescapable fingers to begin drawing her towards the doorway. 'It's impossible to conduct a conversation under these circumstances, and . . .' his white teeth showed in a lazily mocking smile, 'it's not as if I don't know what you look like beneath that filmy creation.'

Unfortunately, the knowledge did not make Jenna feel any less mortified as she was pulled inexorably into the dim, but decidedly more revealing, light of the bedroom, and immediately she felt a slight lessening of his grip she frantically jerked free and rushed to sit on the end of the bed where the already folded quilt thankfully provided her with a little more protection as she dragged it about her hastily. Although not before she had been subjected to an even more encompassing appraisal than the last, and which left her feeling discomposingly hot and flustered.

'So wh-what about Kent?' she faltered, unable to meet his amused gaze. Actually, she would rather have ordered him out of her room altogether, but apprehension had her pressing on, albeit reluctantly.

'I was just wondering if there was some message you may have wanted me to pass on to him for you.'

Jenna drew a deep breath, her eyes flashing with a silvery light as her ire rose at the indisputably facetious offer. 'Mmm, you can tell him I love him, I miss him, and that I can't wait until we're married!' she flared, flippantly sarcastic.

Whatever the reaction she had expected, it wasn't the taunting smile that etched its way across Lane's firmly moulded mouth as he paced silently closer on bare feet and, spanning her jaw abruptly with a strong hand, tilted her startled face upwards.

'Nevertheless, you *are* going to have to wait, my pet,' he insisted. 'And especially since having already willingly spent two nights under your husband's roof . . . as can be corroborated by witnesses. That's hardly likely to convince the court we've separated, now is it?'

'But—but that was because of work!' she gasped. 'As your so-called witnesses can also testify!'

'Not if there should also happen to be more—er—specific evidence as well, though.' Despite the accompanying smile, there was an underlying current of some indefinable emotion in his voice that aroused faint flutterings of alarm in her stomach and had her pulling away from him uneasily.

'But as there's no likelihood of anything else occurring, I doubt either of my visits here will affect the outcome of any divorce proceedings one way or the other!' she contended as she slid her feet to the floor and moved away from him, hauling the quilt with her. 'And now, if you've finished with your little jokes for the night, I'd like you to leave!' Her head angled challengingly.

Lane flexed his powerfully muscled shoulders impassively and half turned, but instead of heading towards the door he began pacing unhurriedly in Jenna's direction, his commanding figure seeming to fill the room the nearer he came and the unnerving sensation of being stalked had her licking at her lips nervously as she backed away.

'Oh, but I wasn't joking,' he demurred softly. 'And I did warn you that I wouldn't be making a divorce easy for you, didn't I?'

Suddenly finding the wall at her back, Jenna clutched at the quilt even more tightly and retaliated defiantly, 'And I'm warning *you*, Lane! Get out of here and leave me alone or I'll make you sorry you didn't, believe me!'

'In what way?' Indolently mocking eyes locked with dilating grey.

Forcing her gaze away, Jenna chanced to see the heavy pottery ashtray on the bedside table next to her and she grabbed at it swiftly. 'This way!' she threatened, holding it aloft.

His ensuing complacent laugh had her carrying out the threat immediately and hurling it at him, but at such close range he evaded it with a consummate ease she found doubly infuriating, and it clattered to the floor behind him, unheeded. Really starting to feel worried now as to his intentions, she lunged for the only weapon left to her, the lamp, but as if sensing her objective Lane caught hold of her arm before she could reach it. Reefing away the protective quilt, he pulled her hard up against his rugged frame, one hand pushing into her silky hair while his other arm encircled her slender form tightly.

'In what way?' he reiterated in the same taunting manner as he trailed his lips across her cheek and then brushed them lightly over own.

Jenna did not even deign to answer this time, but began struggling furiously. 'Stop it, Lane! Let go of me!' she ordered fierily. 'I'm in no mood for playing games with you tonight!'

'So who's playing games?' he countered on a hardening note. 'After tonight you can expect to wait at least another couple of years before you can apply for a divorce on the grounds of separation.'

'*You wouldn't want to try!*'

'Wouldn't I?'

'You do and I'll claw you to pieces!' she vowed desperately.

'You can try, my pet, for all the good it will do you,' he smiled down at her goadingly, ominously.

Jenna renewed her struggles violently. 'Don't feel too sure of yourself, Lane!' she panted. 'I—I'll . . .'

His mouth effectively cut off her words as it closed over hers, hard and possessive, and totally ravishing in its effect. He was relentlessly robbing her of coherent thought, just as he had always been able to do! she suddenly realised in despair, and with her arms trapped securely against her sides she couldn't even implement her last threat in an attempt to force him into releasing her. In a last ditch effort she kicked out at him savagely, but with bare feet it was a futile exercise, and with a disturbing lack of effort Lane swept her off her feet and on to the bed.

Pinning her hands above her head with only one of his own, and her wildly squirming body beneath the muscular length of his, he undid the shoulder ties of her nightdress deftly and guided the transparent material downwards. Jenna gave a panicking gasp, her lissom form twisting even more fiercely, and tried to dig her nails into the hand that was imprisoning hers. By simply re-positioning her wrists Lane made it an impossibility, his free hand then returning to its leisurely exploration of her curving shape, sending uncontrollable tremors of awareness racing through her when it caressed and cupped each of her full breasts in turn. At last he relinquished her lips, but only it seemed in order to stimulate her errant senses with even greater intensity as his mouth and tongue proceeded to tease rosy nipples, already sensitized and throbbing from the attentions of his arousing fingers, to a wanton prominence.

'No!' Jenna sobbed in a combination of anger and

desire, hating the ease with which he could stir her into responding, and despising herself for wanting him to continue inflaming those very same unruly emotions.

'Why not?' Lane raised his head to glance down at her with smouldering eyes, his breathing as harsh and ragged as her own. 'You can't tell me you don't want me as much as I want you!'

'No, I don't! *I don't!*' She shook her head frantically in denial.

'We'll see about that!' he rasped thickly and claimed her quivering lips yet again in a deepening kiss that systematically set about destroying the last of her frail defences.

In the hope of salvaging at least some of her pride and self-respect, Jenna tried resisting to the end, but to her humiliation even that was denied her as she alternately fought against his eventual total possession, and then accepted it fervently, her body betraying her with each rhythmic movement as it arched against him in unreserved rapture.

Much to her surprise that she could have fallen asleep at all, let alone with such apparent speed, when she awakened a couple of hours later Jenna found herself held fast within a pair of strong arms and her head nestled against a smooth, tanned shoulder. Beside the bed the lamp was still burning—evidence that sleep had overtaken Lane swiftly too?—and moving slightly she allowed her eyes to rove over his still features with the aid of its subdued light.

In sleep his face was relaxed, the natural curve of his shapely mouth turning upwards, his brow unfurrowed, his long dark lashes throwing shadows across his cheekbones. Beneath the sheet she was conscious of the warm hardness of his flesh pressed close against hers, their legs still entwined, and uttering an oddly untroubled sigh she lowered her head to his shoulder again.

The movement must have roused Lane because his eyes opened abruptly, instantly alert, their gaze dark and disturbing as they settled on her upturned and sleep-flushed countenance. Jenna ran the tip of her tongue over her lips shakily, knowing herself to be succumbing to the desire visible in his eyes as her hand began smoothing its way over his deep chest to rest tentatively against his lean jaw. With a smothered groan, he rolled on to his side, then propping himself on one elbow looked down at her, waiting for an answer to the unspoken question contained in his fervent glance, until she slid her arms willingly around his neck and pulled his dark head down to hers.

This time they made love with a tenderness and passion reminiscent of the early days of their marriage, and with none of the resistance or the resulting need to exert a male dominance that had been present such a short time before. Now Jenna's responses came uninhibitedly as she savoured his rediscovery of her pliant body, and in turn her exploration of the vital masculinity of his. For his part Lane appeared no less affected as she moulded herself to him invitingly, both their movements becoming more feverish as their desires mounted to seemingly unbearable heights, only to reach even higher and more ecstatic ones when their eager union brought them to a shuddering, exhilarating climax.

In the warm, drowsy afterglow of their love-making Lane drew her close to his side, and with her soft lips shaping contentedly Jenna fitted herself to his sinewed frame compliantly. And why not? she smiled to herself as her eyelids began to droop. He was still her husband, and as those last absorbing minutes had unquestionably showed, she still loved him, didn't she?

Jenna returned to consciousness slowly in the morning, stretching sinuously as she recalled the events of the night before, and then smiling ruefully on finding she had the bed to herself. Nothing ever prevented Lane from rising early! Well, almost nothing, she amended with an irrepressible grin.

Lying back on her pillow, she remembered her last thought before falling asleep, her mind mulling over it unhurriedly. Although the realisation had surfaced when she had been feeling too languid to even question it, she now found in the full light of day that it was no more than the truth. She did still love her husband! And as deeply, as achingly, and as totally as she ever had, no matter what she may have persuaded herself into thinking otherwise during the last five years, she acknowledged with a not unhappy sigh.

Now she knew why she had always been so reluctant to put into motion the law suit that would have irrevocably separated them, and why Lane had been able to create such a disconcerting feeling of attraction within her at times lately. It also explained the reason she had avoided informing Kent of her continuing marriage for so long, she supposed, and why his embraces had never really seemed to arouse anything other than surface emotions. There had only ever been one man in her life, would only ever be one man in her life, and she had merely been fooling herself by pretending anyone else could ever supplant him.

And after those final rapturous moments of last night it surely meant that Lane felt the same towards her! she hazarded gaily, throwing off the sheet and sliding from the bed quickly. An excited expectancy at the thought of seeing him again was suddenly gripping her and she didn't want to waste another minute before seeking his vibrant company.

Showering and dressing hastily in a flattering, figure-hugging top and lemon shorts, Jenna's eyes sparkled as she descended the stairs with a light step and made her way to the patio. Her excitement being dampened somewhat on finding no one there and the table only set for one.

'Oh, Miss Bowman, you're up.' Enid Squires came bustling out of the kitchen on noticing her. 'What would you like for breakfast?'

As food was the last thing on her mind, Jenna half shrugged vaguely. 'Oh—er—coffee and toast, that's all, thank you, Mrs Squires.' Then, looking about her searchingly, hopefully, 'Where's Lane? Has he finished his already?'

'Oh, my word, yes,' came the half smiled answer. 'In fact, he left to visit Miss Cornell over an hour ago. He asked me to tell you, though, that as he would be going straight to the airport afterwards there was no need for you to ruin your Saturday by waiting for him, and that he would see you in the office on Wednesday.'

'I see.' Jenna bit at her lip sharply to stop its sudden trembling as wave upon wave of desolation crashed over her and the glow in her eyes died. 'And—and is that all he said?' she still had to ask, jerkily.

The housekeeper frowned, looking at her strangely. 'Why, is there something important he's missed? I have Miss Cornell's number if you need to contact him.'

'No, it's nothing of importance,' Jenna denied bitterly. How could it be? Lane had told her plainly enough why he had taken her to bed. She had just stupidly blinded herself to the fact. And if she needed any further proof that their final love-making had meant absolutely nothing to him, his seeking Rosalind Cornell's arms immediately after leaving her bed was incontrovertible.

'Well, if you're sure, I'll just get your breakfast, then,' Enid Squires said and headed back to the kitchen.

Left on her own, Jenna sank on to a chair at the table with her eyes stinging saltily and her emotions more raw and lacerated than they had been at the time of her marriage break-up. No need to ruin her day by waiting for him he had said! Oh, God, with one premeditated stroke he had successfully ruined the rest of her life! she came close to sobbing.

When the housekeeper brought out her breakfast, Jenna thanked her huskily, the hard lump that seemed to have settled in her throat making speech almost impossible, and although she did manage to force down a little of the coffee, the toast she could not face at all. Her entire being was now concentrated on leaving the place as soon as she could—together with the agonising memories it evoked—and it was not long before she had collected her belongings from the room she never wanted to see again, as well as her notes and papers from the office, and bidden goodbye to Mrs Squires.

Damn him, damn him, *damn him*! she cursed brokenly as she walked out into the sun-splashed forecourt. No doubt he had only stayed with her in order that his housekeeper would note his bed had not been slept in and would consequently make the right deduction as to the reasons! Or maybe he had even cunningly arranged for Enid Squires to see him when he emerged from the wrong room in the morning! He had implied more specific evidence regarding their supposedly not being separated could be obtained, hadn't he?

She caught back a small choked sound. But had he really had to make her fall in love with him all over again in achieving his object? she cried despairingly, resentfully, her eyes beginning to fill with tears. And why, oh why, had he had to make love to her as if it had meant something to him? That was perhaps the part that hurt most, and which she found the least possible to forgive. There had been absolutely no necessity for it ... unless, of course, because she had unthinkingly shown herself to be so willing, he had simply accepted what was conveniently on offer due to there being nothing better—in the shape of the amorous Rosalind—at hand!

The idea had a tinge of acrimony mixing with her anguish, followed swiftly by a flood of anger as the notion became more firmly implanted in her mind, and she flung her bag into her car roughly. Surprisingly, Lane's Alpha was angle-parked near hers on the wide sloping driveway, but then she surmised absently that for some reason he must have taken the Range Rover she had noticed in the garage the last time she was there instead. He always had liked going bush whenever the opportunity presented itself.

For a moment Jenna stared at the dark blue vehicle balefully, seeing it only as an extension of its owner, but as an abrupt impulse for reprisal beset her, she walked over to it purposefully. Opening the door, she reached in to shift the gears to neutral and deliberately release the hand brake, then stepping back rapidly, closed the door. The car began to roll almost immediately and she watched with a stony gaze as it gathered speed before first scraping against the garden retaining wall and then crunching solidly into the sandstone rock face opposite with a screech of protesting metal.

Thankfully, Floyd was mowing the lawn on one of the terraces below, the noise of the mower preventing the sound of the car's crash from reaching the house, but now that she had exacted her retaliation Jenna promptly touched her teeth to her lower lip in dismay as her conscience smote her. It was the first time in her life she had ever even contemplated doing anything quite so reprehensibly destructive, and it was—or had been until it suffered the extensive damage she had just inflicted on it!—such a beautiful vehicle.

Not that Lane did not deserve it, of course, she tried to console herself with a defiant toss of her head. When all was said and done, after his heart-wrenching treatment of her, he could not expect to get off entirely unpunished. And—and anyway, he could certainly afford to have it repaired, and not only that, but as he kept insisting she was still his wife—had made her so literally as well as legally last night!—then why couldn't that be her part of the car to do with however she saw fit?

Thus attempting to appease her feelings of guilt, Jenna returned to her own vehicle and set it in motion, although her ensuing flight down the driveway and on to the road was still made as fast as was humanly possible.

CHAPTER SIX

ALTHOUGH Jenna could have driven up to the Blue Mountains to see her parents later on Saturday and then stayed till Sunday, she decided against it, preferring to occupy her time doing vigorous housework at her apartment instead. Now that her parents knew about her meeting Lane again their questions would have been endless, and right at present he was the last person she wanted to think about, let alone discuss.

On Monday and Tuesday she typed up all Lane's dictation and, for a change, was able to go shopping in her lunchtime with Freda. Since her husband took over the office it was something she had not had an opportunity to do, because he had altered the hour of her lunch break due to his own preference for a later one. Wednesday was another matter, however, for even as her mind still seethed with bitterness against Lane's ruthlessly calculating behaviour, every now and then her rancour was superseded by an almost quaking alarm concerning his probable reaction if he should ever discover she had been responsible for the damage done to his car. Of course it was unlikely that he would, she reassured herself encouragingly, because she was sure no one had seen her, but at the same time there was always that agile brain of his to consider. Lane wasn't anyone's fool, and if he should suspect ... Jenna shivered convulsively and set about dispelling the thought by once again remembering her own grievances.

Lane eventually put in an appearance shortly after Jenna had returned from lunch. As it happened she had expected him earlier, for his plane had been due to arrive mid-morning, but deducing the flight must have been late for some reason, or else he had called in at head office on his way to the plant, she watched his long striding approach with surreptitious but condemning eyes. He disappeared into Ian's room for a few minutes before passing her desk, but when he came out the hostile look on his face as it came to rest briefly on her studiously indifferent features had her swallowing nervously.

'*In the office, Jenna!*' he ground out in a savage undertone as he passed her without stopping, and running her suddenly damp palms down the sides of her slim-fitting skirt, she rose to her feet reluctantly and followed him.

Lane waited by the door with his hands resting on his lithe hips for her to enter and then slammed it shut with a force that set the picture on the wall nearest it rattling. He was not just annoyed or angry . . . he was *livid!* she noted warily. Although what about she could not imagine as she doubted he would even have been home yet to learn of the accident that had befallen his car. A comforting thought that enabled her to return his direful gaze with a challenging one of her own. After all, she was the one who had most to complain about, not him!

'Did you have a bad flight?' she therefore saw fit to commiserate with dubious sorrow.

Momentarily, Jenna thought he meant to strike her as he took a menacing step closer. A step she involuntarily copied, backwards, and which did not go unnoticed by definitely threatening eyes.

'Yes, you'd better back off!' he warned harshly. 'And you can forget the play-acting too! You know damn bloody well what's making me ropeable!'

'How could I?' Her gaze turned resentful, but she refused to drop it before his. 'I haven't seen you since you carried out your despicable plan on Saturday night!'

'And that's precisely what's at the bottom of all this, isn't it, Jenna? You just had to wreak your revenge somehow! But weren't you game to try inflicting it on me, personally?' he jeered with scathing contempt.

'I don't know what you're talking about,' she claimed, outwardly calm and defiant. Inside, it was something else again as icy tremors chased up and down her spine. Oh, God, he *did* already know about his car—and had evidently come to the conclusion she most feared!

'Not much, you don't!' His hands found their way on to his hips again. As if to prevent them from encircling her throat! Jenna deduced. 'So you can stop stalling, because I'm in no frame of mind to put up with it! We're talking about my car! The dark blue one . . . remember?'

'Y-your car?' she repeated, deliberately obtuse, although the stammer was genuine enough.

His out-thrust jaw clenched noticeably. 'Yes, my car!' he grated. 'It appears it had an accident on Saturday!'

And she still felt it served him right! 'So what's that supposed to do with me?' she shrugged. 'I wasn't driving it.'

Now Lane did grab hold of her, but thankfully only

by the shoulders, although the violent shaking he gave her she certainly wasn't grateful for. 'No, but you were the one who released the brake and put it out of gear! I'm not such an idiot that I couldn't recognise your hand there, Jenna, so don't make the mistake of trying to treat me as if I am!'

'Oh?' Jenna arched her brows skywards, her own expression beginning to darken somewhat stormily now. 'And why would I do that?'

'As I said, for spite, most probably! Not that you ever seemed to think you needed an excuse for your conduct!'

'Why should I?' She suddenly threw caution to the winds as she remembered the desolation that had swamped her on finding him gone on Saturday morning—and to visit Rosalind, at that. 'I didn't hear you come up with a very good excuse for your behaviour of the night before! So why shouldn't I retaliate in any way I can?'

'*My behaviour?*' He uttered a short bark of corrosive laughter. 'And what about yours? Although you may have offered some slight resistance at first, as I recall you weren't exactly reluctant the second time, my love!'

'Oh, you bastard!' she exploded anguishedly and swung a furious hand towards his face, but which he arrested in a painful grip, not bothering to disguise his overpowering strength. 'Trust a man to make an odious remark like that!'

'And trust a woman to do something outrageous like deliberately smashing an almost brand new car . . . and expect to get away with it as well!' he countered with blistering scorn. 'Well, I just hope you don't find the repayments as outrageous!'

'What repayments?'

'The ones that will be extracted from your wages each week to pay for the necessary repairs!'

Jenna's eyes widened in indignant disbelief. 'You can't expect me to pay for those! It would take me months. You don't exactly pay exorbitant wages, you know!'

'I know precisely how much you're paid, my pet, but that's your problem ... not mine! It may have been better if you'd taken that into consideration before wreaking your revenge in such an extreme fashion!'

'Well, I hardly anticipated having to pay for it, and—and ...' She came to a halt, her breasts heaving with resentment, her mouth setting in a rebellious line. 'And nor do I intend to! You can afford it better than I can.'

'Whether I can or not, has nothing to do with it,' Lane discounted bleakly. 'Because you either pay for the work that needs doing, or I make an official complaint for malicious damage to private property!'

'You wouldn't!'

'Oh, no?'

'Against you own *wife*?'

His well-defined brows lifted expressively. 'Ah, but as you're so fond of saying, you're not my wife, are you, *Miss* Bowman? You can hardly claim that distinction just when you feel like it, Jenna, or whenever you think it may prove advantageous.'

'Well, you certainly didn't have any qualms about taking advantage of being my husband the other night!' she flared.

'Mmm, but then you shouldn't keep flaunting your desire for a divorce at me, otherwise I may be tempted to do the same again,' he returned arrogantly, impenitently.

So that was all it had meant to him. 'You'll never get the chance, Lane, you can be sure of that!' Her voice shook with the effort to convince him, as well as to hide her suffocating sense of despair.

He shrugged imperturbably, his mouth assuming a mocking slant. 'From what I saw of Sharman, that could be unnecessary, anyway.'

'Meaning?'

'He appears rather—er—taken with an attractive brunette in his new office,' he drawled.

Jenna struggled to keep her expression impassive. Whether it was the truth or not—it could just have been a ploy to hopefully create friction between Kent and herself—it really did not matter any more after last weekend had devastatingly brought home to her in just which direction her true feelings lay. However, for her own protection she obviously had to continue pretending otherwise.

'A friendship you, no doubt, did your best to foster,' she charged on a steady note. Even if she had believed herself to still be in love with Kent, she would not have wanted to give her husband the satisfaction of thinking his statement had caused her any distress.

Lane hunched his wide shoulders again, as if the matter was of little concern to him. 'I didn't engineer their meeting, if that's what you're thinking,' he advised wryly.

'Except indirectly, of course!' The bittersweet gibe was out before she could halt it, and she promptly set about adding a defensive rejoinder. 'That is, if there *is* any such attraction on Kent's part!'

'Oh, there's something there all right,' he was not averse to assuring her. 'Anyone with half an eye could see that, and I'm sure not the only one who's noticed it.'

Jenna pressed her lips together indecisively, unsure as to how she should reply in order to give the impression she was not upset, yet without making him suspicious as to just why the news had not affected her as much as he evidently anticipated, or wanted. Unwittingly, it was Lane who came to her aid.

'Surprise, huh?' he goaded.

'Wasn't it meant to be?' The touch of acid in her tone was not faked.

His expression indicated indifference, but she was not fooled. 'So what do you intend doing now?'

'Getting on with my work . . . if that's acceptable to you,' she returned glibly. Not for anything would she reveal she intended doing nothing about Kent's apparent defection.

Her tacit insinuation that it was none of his business had her undergoing a measuring glance for a minute and then he half tilted his head as if losing interest. 'It could be best,' he granted. 'Otherwise you might be wanting to work overtime in order to catch up and at those rates it could be cheaper for me to pay for the repairs to my car myself.' His lips twitched tauntingly.

The reminder had Jenna aiming him a fulminating glare and making her exit with as resounding a slam of the door as he had executed when she entered.

However, as week followed week and Kent's communications gradually became more stilted as their frequency decreased, it was soon obvious that his interest was, as Lane had implied, becoming centred elsewhere. A circumstance Jenna accepted with relief actually. Feeling as she did about her husband again, despite their seemingly endless verbal confrontations, it would have been impossible for her to continue with their relationship, and at least this way their association could come to an end without her having to dissemble as to the reasons why she wanted to make the break.

With no one to distract her thoughts from Lane now, though, and especially when her hours of work began resuming a more regular pattern as less re-organisation was required to maintain the company's steady improvement, it became increasingly difficult for her to put her husband out of her mind for any length of time and, in consequence, she started to give serious consideration to leaving the firm after all.

Since Lane appeared in no hurry to return to head office, she doubted her ability to successfully disguise for much longer the depressing anguish that always seemed to assail her while in his disturbing presence without him sensing the cause for her uncustomarily subdued behaviour—not even the exasperating smile he bestowed on her every pay day when she grudgingly handed over the requisite repayments for his car induced more than a briefly reproachful glance in response nowadays—and she looked forward to the approaching Christmas holidays she intended spending with her parents as a welcome interlude in which to make her final decision.

Nevertheless, when they did finally arrive they were not nearly as conducive to logical reasoning as Jenna had hoped because her parents were, unknowingly, all too effective in not allowing her to exclude Lane from her thoughts, even temporarily or partially, as their interested questions regarding him constantly defeated her. What also made it harder was the fact that, subconsciously anyway, she knew she did not want to take that final step that would physically put him out of her life—being able to see him was at least better than nothing—but then, towards the end of the week even that problem paled into insignificance beside the one that now came to torment her.

The first morning she felt distinctly queasy after breakfast she attributed to a slight over-indulgence in both food and wine at the party her parents had given for some of their friends and neighbours the night before, but when after a day or two she was again plagued by identical feelings and on two consecutive mornings which had not been preceded by any such festivities, she realised that the previous signs she had tried so hard to rationalise, and thereby ignore, were now making themselves impossible to disclaim. She was pregnant! And by a husband whose only desire to retain their married state was as a barrier against any of his female companions who might show an inclination for a trip to the altar! If it had not been so lacerating, Jenna may have found it laughable, but as it was all she could do was worry. Abortion was out of the question, she wanted the baby too much for that. Even if Lane did not want her, she wanted his child with every fibre of her being, particularly after their first had—had . . . She forced her thoughts back to her most pressing problem.

How on earth was she going to provide a good home life for the baby and yet keep working full time as well? She supposed she could return to her parents' home permanently and apply for a position in one of the larger nearby towns—Katoomba, or Penrith, perhaps? Her mother would be more than willing to care for the baby during the day for her, she knew, and yet at the same time she did not think it really fair to put such a burden on her parents at their age. The more so when she was as well aware they would feel that, under such circumstances, her place really should have been with her husband.

As far as Jenna was concerned, however, she did not even intend to inform Lane she was expecting a baby at all. Partly, because she did not feel the reason for the baby's existence even entitled him to know, but also because she just could not be certain what his reaction might be if he did discover she was pregnant. There was always the chance he might decide to exact a little more revenge of his own by attempting to take the child from her once it was born—he was certainly in a position to provide for one better than she, and her parents combined, ever could—and the idea had her close to tears just thinking about it. Why did everything always seem to work in his favour? she cried helplessly.

But on returning to work after New Year, Jenna unfortunately found her pregnancy not such an easy secret to keep, harassed as she was by a morning sickness that uncooperatively did not always confine its appearance to early in the day but would often arrive at other inopportune moments as well! Freda was the first to guess the truth when a hasty departure from the staff room during morning tea had been necessitated two days in a row.

'I know it's nothing to do with me, but would I be right in thinking you're expecting?' she enquired on the younger girl's return, the others already having left.

With a sigh, Jenna sank on to the chair next to her,

her lips twisting wryly. 'I guess it's becoming somewhat obvious, isn't it?'

Freda half smiled and nodded. 'Kent?' she deduced.

Jenna shifted uncomfortably. 'No.'

The other girl's surprise showed in her widening eyes. 'Th-then who?' she stammered incredulously.

'I—umm—it's a long story,' Jenna faltered, but because she did not want Freda thinking it was the result of a casual affair, reluctantly proceeded to explain as briefly as possible, although careful to omit the name of the man to whom she was still married.

'I see,' Freda acknowledged thoughtfully when she had finished. 'So what will you do?'

'Continue working here for as long as it doesn't show and then inflict myself on Mum and Dad, I guess,' Jenna proposed on a rueful note.

'Oh, but you could continue working longer than that if you wanted to. I'm sure no one here would mind,' put forward Freda earnestly. 'Why don't you ask your boss about it?'

Jenna swallowed heavily. 'I—I'll think about it,' she parried. It was easier than attempting to explain an outright refusal.

'Well, if there's anything I can do,' said Freda sympathetically as she began rising to her feet, 'just let me know, okay?'

'Thanks,' Jenna smiled sincerely. 'But at the moment I'd just like it kept between ourselves, if possible.'

Freda nodded understandingly and they left the room together, Jenna collecting her notebook and pencil as they parted at her desk, and then heading for Lane's office. He only managed to dictate two letters before she felt beads of perspiration starting to break out on her forehead and although she fought the feeling of rising nausea for as long as she was able, eventually she had no choice but to utter a hasty apology and hurriedly seek the amenities of the ladies' room once more.

Nor did she feel very much better on her return some minutes later, and particularly when she intercepted Lane's lowering gaze on resuming her seat opposite him.

'I'm sorry,' she apologised weakly again. And surmising it might be prudent to provide some sort of excuse, offered, 'I think I must have eaten something last night that didn't agree with me.'

'Oh?' One dark brow quirked upwards. 'The night before too?'

Jenna's throat tightened. 'I don't know what you mean.'

'I mean, word gets around in offices this size, and the word is that you weren't feeling very bright yesterday either!'

Drops of perspiration made a reappearance at her temples. 'Yes—well—maybe . . .'

'Maybe . . . nothing!' he broke in on her sardonically. 'Don't try playing me for a fool, Jenna! You forget, I've been through all this before, and it's got nothing to do with anything you've eaten! You're just plain pregnant!' His eyes filled with derisive sarcasm. 'Aren't you, my love?'

And she had thought to keep it a secret! Her head tilted to an unconsciously defiant angle. 'And if I am?'

'Then you evidently should have been more careful,' he mocked.

'So should you!' she was stung into retorting. That he could make so light of his part in the matter was incredible!

'Me?' He gave a ridiculing laugh. 'Oh, no, my pet, you're not landing me with someone else's offspring just because you've got yourself in a fix by being married to one and sleeping with another ... whose interest has now been diverted!'

For a moment Jenna experienced a sense of relief that he did not believe the child she was carrying was his—it made matters so much more simple—but then she knew she could not allow him to go on thinking that way, not only for his child's sake and Kent's, but her own as well.

'I wasn't sleeping with Kent,' she denied urgently. 'But even you can't pretend I didn't sleep with *you*!'

He smiled, ironically. 'Although I can pretend to know that one night's love-making doesn't automatically produce progeny!' He paused, his mouth firming inflexibly. 'And especially when I have it on your own admission that you and Sharman believed in a sexual relationship!'

She remembered the occasion well. 'But I only said that because you were trying to make me look like some old-fashioned prude in front of your girl-friend!'

'And the morning after the conference when you were explaining how such activities kept the pair of you awake so late at night? Was that for the same reason too?' he quizzed satirically, disbelievingly.

She recalled that all too well also, but ... 'I didn't say that exactly,' she protested, albeit not very strongly. It was a little difficult when that had been the impression she had attempted to convey at the time. 'I said our talking kept us up late.'

'Mmm, body talk, no doubt!'

The utterly unconvinced look on his face had her sighing defeatedly and shaking her head. 'All right, if that's the way you want it,' she shrugged wearily. At least she had tried, and despite originally neither intending, nor wanting to.

Momentarily, it appeared as if Lane had something to add, but then he too shrugged and agreed, 'That's the way I want it.'

In a way Jenna felt grateful as it meant her worst fear—that he might at some time make an effort to seek custody of the child—would never eventuate. A thought so heartening that she felt as if a great load had been lifted from her and enabling her to make definite plans for both the baby's and her own future now without hindrance. Something she was still musing happily over that evening when a knock on her door advised she had a visitor.

When she discovered it was Lane standing on the threshold—although not for long as he yet again strode past her without waiting for an invitation—she was suddenly filled with apprehension, but struggling valiantly not to show it as she turned to face him.

'Well?' she demanded indignantly.

He did not immediately answer, but made himself more at home by relaxing comfortably on her sofa, his arms reaching out on either side of him along the back, the ankle of one long leg resting casually on his opposite knee.

'I just came to advise that your resignation has been accepted, Mrs Forrester,' he finally drawled in whimsical tones.

Jenna's breathing quickened rapidly and for a time his mode of address went unnoticed as all her attention was concentrated on what had preceded it. 'Oh, you—you swine!' she blazed fiercely. 'This is another of your ideas of retaliation, isn't it? You knew I'd be needing the money so you just couldn't wait to fire me, you callous reptile!'

'And you're so busy jumping to conclusions that you don't even bother to listen, you spitting virago!' he retorted in similar fashion, although rather more sarcastically than heatedly. 'So why don't you just calm down and pay attention for once, hmm?'

'Why should I?' she heaved mutinously.

His shapely mouth crooked wryly. 'Because you may hear something that concerns you.'

'Such as why I'm being fired?' she gibed.

'I said I'd accepted your resignation, not that I was dismissing you!'

'The result's the same, isn't it?' She eyed him bitterly.

'If by that you mean, you won't be working any more, then I suppose the answer is yes,' he conceded.

'Precisely as I thought!'

'Except for the reason, Mrs Forrester.' He repeated the name again and this time it registered.

'And just what are you trying to imply by that?' she queried suspiciously.

'I didn't realise it could mean more than one thing,' Lane smiled drily. Then, before she could reply, 'I rang Sharman tonight.'

'Oh, no!' Jenna couldn't prevent the shocked gasp from escaping, her grey eyes shading with dismay.

'Mmm, that's more or less what he said when I told him you were expecting and asked what he intended doing about it,' he relayed with a hint of sardonic amusement.

She shook her head helplessly. 'Oh, God, why did you have to do that?' she cried.

'Because I considered it the best way to discover the truth!' she was informed on a roughening note.

'You mean, you believed anything he had to say?' He hadn't anything she had said!

His lips took on an oblique slant. 'Oh, yes, his outrage at the thought of you choosing to sleep with someone else when you apparently wouldn't with him was obviously genuine.'

'And?' she prompted dully.

'I'm willing to accept now that the child you're carrying is mine.'

At that her eyes darkened stormily. 'My, that is magnanimous of you!' she sniped. 'You're sure there's not been anyone else in my life whose offspring I'm attempting to land you with?'

Lane rose to his feet in a smoothly agile action, his hands catching her by the shoulders and determinedly remaining there when she would have pulled away. 'Yes, I'm sure, and—and I'm sorry if I didn't word that as well as you would have wanted or as I could have, and even for disbelieving you today, but . . .,' he sighed and dragged a hand through his short hair, 'as you damned well know, there were extenuating circumstances surrounding that. You'd deliberately led me to think you and Sharman were having an affair.'

Jenna half raised a shoulder in a vaguely acknow-ledging movement, her gaze downcast as it fastened to her tightly intertwining fingers. 'I still don't see what any of this has to do with me leaving work,' she claimed moodily.

'Because there's no necessity for you to continue any more, of course,' was the faintly impatient return. 'It's about time you reverted to your proper name, anyway, isn't it?'

'I don't see the connection,' she looked up with a frown.

'The connection is, my love, that like it or not, you *are* my wife, and while you're carrying my child and living in my home . . .'

'No!' she interrupted with a vehement protest, shaking her head wildly. 'I may be expecting your child, Lane, but there's no way I'll ever live with you again!' It was too soul-destroying to contemplate being accepted only because of the baby they had inadvertently conceived. If she did not love him, maybe she could have resigned herself to it, but as it was even the idea was intolerable! 'We're separated, and we're going to remain that way! Besides, I—I've already made my plans.'

'Such as?' His voice hardened markedly.

'I'm going back to live with Mum and Dad,' she strove to impress him with her conviction.

His thickly lashed eyes narrowed watchfully. 'I didn't think they were in a position to support another two.'

'No—well—once the baby's born I—I'll get another position,' she advanced anxiously. 'Mum will look after . . .'

'The hell she will!' His unconditional veto sliced through her theory ruthlessly. 'As good a job as I'm sure your mother would do with the child, there's no way this child is going to be reared by anyone but its rightful parents and in its rightful home! And that means you and I together, my pet, in *our* home! Or were you just hoping to delegate your responsibilities in that area yet again?' he jeered contemptuously.

'No! And—and you have no right to—to imply anything so hateful,' she choked as she bit at her lip to stop its hurt quivering. She released a shuddering breath. 'In any case, it's *your* home, not ours!'

'It will be when you're living there too!'

Under sufferance? She moved her head dismally. 'It wouldn't work, Lane, it just wouldn't work! We'd only fight all the time again, and that's no atmosphere for a child to live in.'

'Then we'll just have to make an effort to ensure the atmosphere improves, won't we?' There was no sign of any relenting in his voice. 'And you must have known this would be the outcome when you tried to convince me of my part in the matter earlier.'

Actually, she had not been thinking that far ahead at the time. 'No, since you'd realised I was pregnant I just thought it wasn't fair to the baby not to be acknowledged by its true father, or for Kent to be accused of something he didn't do,' she disclosed in a murmur.

Lane's head inclined speculatively. 'Not to keep the record straight regarding you as well?'

Jenna partly turned away. As far as the hands still capturing her shoulders would allow. 'That too, I guess,' she admitted with an offhandedness she hoped would hide just how much it had really meant to her.

'You should have known better.'

Her eyes closed anguishedly. Meaning, he already thought the worst of her, anyway, she supposed. With an effort she made herself face him again.

'You don't think that's sufficient reason for us to remain separated?' she half laughed with shaky irony.

His brows pulled together sharply. 'You're not making sense!'

'I think I am.'

'Hmm . . .' One side of his mouth suddenly swept upwards. 'And somehow I get the feeling you've been jumping to conclusions again.' Removing a hand from her shoulder he spanned her jaw and tilted her head up to his. 'So what bee have you got in your bonnet this time, eh?'

'Don't make fun of me, Lane!' she flared and slapped his hand away. 'I *know* the way you think!'

'Then as I said, you really should have known better than to think that under the circumstances I wouldn't insist on you returning to live in my home, shouldn't you?' he mocked.

'Oh!' Jenna flushed self-consciously as her spirits abruptly lifted. Was that what he'd meant? Not that it had her changing her mind, though. 'Yes, well, you can insist all you like, but I still have no intention of . . .'

'And I don't give a damn about your intentions!' Lane overrode her arrogantly. 'That's an absurd scenario you've decided upon, and if you weren't such a wilful, self-pitying little vixen you'd admit it! Now . . .' his eyes blazed down into hers remorselessly, 'do you start doing your packing, or do I?'

Her desire to object to his last arbitrary dictate was submerged momentarily beneath a seething resentment. 'I'm surprised you would even want me in your house if that's how you feel about me,' she gibed, her expression stiff in her attempt to keep it uncaring.

'Yeah, well, we all have a cross to bear, don't we?' he drawled caustically.

'And your forbearance is positively overwhelming!' she promptly snapped back.

'While you're not doing any packing!' He referred to his original instruction meaningfully.

Feeling as if she was being forced into a corner from which there would be no escape, Jenna tried to evade it frantically. 'But why do I have to move right now?'

she queried on a protesting note. 'Why not in a few months or so? *If* I have to do so at all!'

'Because it's not going to take long for everyone in that office to make the same deduction as I did concerning those bouts of nausea of yours, my love, and I rather think it will be less embarrassing all round if it's known we're married before that happens rather than afterwards,' he proposed sardonically. 'It's going to create enough talk as it is and I suspect you may find it somewhat less of an ordeal if you stay well clear of it and leave me to do the explaining.'

He did have a point, Jenna conceded grudgingly and sighed. It appeared she had reached that corner after all, and with a grimace she headed for her bedroom to begin packing.

CHAPTER SEVEN

FOR Jenna, living in Lane's house was purgatory. Being so near to him physically, but so far estranged from him in every other way, was a sorrow-laden torment she just could not come to grips with and which had her retreating further and further within herself as each day passed. For a while she had been hopeful that, by some strange miracle, it might work out, but when it became obvious Lane intended to maintain the politely distant attitude he had adopted towards her since she moved in she knew she had only been wishing for the unattainable. Having succeeded in excercising his husbandly rights by installing her in his home, his only interest in her now was as the future mother of his unborn child.

To Jenna's surprise, the most kindly person towards her had been Mrs Squires who, although evincing some amazement on learning that Jenna was the wife Lane had been parted from for so long, but which Jenna still surmised she had suspected for quite some time, was at least prepared to try and make her feel less of a visitor whose presence was merely tolerated. Even so, Jenna found the days interminably long as she waited with involuntary expectancy for her husband to return each night; only to have him forsake her company as soon as he civilly could in order to retire to the downstairs office, to go back to work, to see Floyd about some matter concerning the house or grounds that required attention—in fact to go anywhere where she wasn't! she noted with mounting misery.

The last straw was when Rosalind Cornell paid a visit, at a time when she would have been well aware Lane was not at home, and as a result had Jenna greeting her warily when the housekeeper showed the stunningly outfitted woman into the sitting-room where she had been occupying herself with some knitting for the baby in order to pass the time. Wearing an extremely fashionable dress of the palest of rose-pink silk, complemented by a choker of pearls that Jenna hazarded must have cost a fortune, and perfectly matching darker rose accessories, there was no denying that she looked fabulous. But it was just as evident the older woman knew it too, as she sauntered imperiously into the room and responded condescendingly to Jenna's greeting before taking the seat proffered.

'Well, you are a sly one, and no mistake, aren't you?' she slighted under cover of a smile that did not reach her frosty-hued eyes. 'But as Lane and I are such . . .' she hesitated explicitly, 'good friends, I thought it only right that I should become acquainted with his wife too.'

Jenna lifted her head fractionally. 'That *is* considerate of you,' she returned, facetiously tongue-in-cheek.

'Well, you know how it is,' Rosalind waved a perfectly manicured hand blithely. 'Everyone's known Lane's been married for years, of course, but to suddenly discover his wife's none other than his new little secretary who's now ensconced in his home— and pregnant too, I hear—well, you can imagine our surprise!' She paused, her expression sharpening maliciously. 'Since Lane's always been too busy to seek a divorce I suppose you had no choice but to beg him to give your child a name when you found out, and being as easy-going as he is, he agreed.'

Jenna's blood pressure rose uncontrollably, and it was only with some effort that she managed to remain seated instead of rushing across the room to deal with the smirking blonde as she felt like doing. 'Not at all,' she denied with a forced little laugh of mocking amusement. 'I mean, who else's name but Lane's would you expect a child of his to have?'

'You're saying . . .?' For a moment Rosalind's jaw dropped and then it closed again with a snap. 'And he admits it?'

'Naturally,' Jenna enjoyed confirming. 'In fact, it was at his insistence that we're living together again.' And deciding a little more salt in the evident wound would not go amiss, 'He's very family minded, you know.'

'He certainly hasn't been for the last two years!' Rosalind obviously just could not help bursting out in rancorous tones. Then recovering quickly she fixed her self assured smile firmly in place once more. 'Although, in your case, I suppose he has to at least make an attempt to keep up appearances.'

The remark was too near the truth and Jenna felt a sharp stab of pain in her chest. 'Quite successfully, though. I would have said,' she just managed to get out.

'Oh, I don't know.' Rosalind's smile became more barbed as she sensed a victory. 'I haven't noticed I've seen any less of him since your arrival on—or should I say return to?—the scene.'

Jenna sucked in a steadying breath to help overcome the feeling of wretchedness that swept over her.

'Probably because I'm his wife, not his watchdog,' she tried to make light of it. 'He's free to come and go as he pleases.'

'Then he obviously pleases to go more often than not, doesn't he?' Rosalind was swift to retort with a taunting smile. 'And as you must have realised that day in Lane's office when you interrupted us so awkwardly, really you're very much *de trop*, sweetie. That means—unwanted, in the way, unwelcome,' she elucidated in patronising, unsparing tones.

Jenna dipped her head jerkily. 'Thank you, I did know what it meant.'

'Oh, dear, now I've upset you!' Rosalind exclaimed with false concern. 'Which really wasn't my intention at all. I simply wanted to point out to you that even though Lane is now acknowledging you as his wife, and apparently only because he thoughtlessly made use of you—men can be so free and easy like that at times, can't they?' she inserted in a pseudo-friendly manner, 'it doesn't mean he intends to end our association. That will still continue, and you'll only be hurting yourself if you're deluded enough to imagine otherwise. After all, Lane and I have a great deal in common—business, friends, aspirations—and even you must know you just don't fit in, sweetie. Why, look at you now, *knitting* baby clothes, for heaven's sake!' She gave a low, disparaging laugh. 'Lane would expect any child of his to wear better clothes than poorly home-made ones, I'm sure.'

Although she would dearly have loved to order the insulting woman from the house, Jenna just was not sure what her husband's reaction would be if she did. Since it had been impressed on her before that Rosalind Cornell was a highly valued client—among other things!—the repercussions from such an action might only serve to alienate Lane even further and she did not want to take a chance on that happening. Fortunately, though, help was to come from another quarter as Enid Squires suddenly appeared in the doorway.

'I'm sorry to interrupt, Mrs Forrester,' she began formally, which was surprising in itself considering they had been on first name terms for a week or more now, 'but I thought I'd better remind you that you have that appointment at the clinic at eleven, and it's ten-thirty now.'

For a moment Jenna stared back at her blankly—she did not have an appointment at the clinic this week!—and then she heaved a grateful sigh and gained her feet rapidly. The housekeeper was thoughtfully providing her with an excuse to get rid of her unwanted visitor.

'Why, thank you, Mrs Squires,' she smiled at the older woman. 'I had forgotten all about it, actually.' She turned to the silver blonde who was still seated. 'I'm sorry to have to cut our so very informative conversation short, but . . .' She spread her hands meaningfully wide. 'If you'll excuse me?'

Rosalind could hardly refuse, but it was in noticeable vexation that she rose upright. 'Yes, well, I suppose we'll just have to finish it some other time,' she conceded, asperity predominant.

Not if Jenna could help it! 'Oh, I don't really think that will be necessary. I'm sure I understand your position quite clearly now,' she advised with a flippancy she was far from feeling.

'Well, at least that's something!' Rosalind contended as she began moving towards the door. 'Perhaps we'll meet again at some social function or the other, then. *If* Lane's disposed to bring you, of course!'

Her parting shot had Jenna shaking her head wearily. Rosalind Cornell was the most tiring, and tiresome, woman she had ever come across, and when the housekeeper returned from seeing her out she greeted her appreciatively.

'I can't thank you enough, Enid,' she averred devoutly. 'I'm afraid Miss Cornell is just a little too overpowering at close range.'

'Mmm, I thought she might be giving you a hard time,' Enid nodded understandingly. 'She's a very formidable lady, that one, and she labours under the unfortunate belief that whatever Miss Cornell wants, Miss Cornell is entitled to get.'

'And right at the moment she wants my husband,' Jenna murmured disconsolately. She did not doubt for one minute that Enid was not as aware of the fact as she was.

'Mmm, that's been her ambition all right, but now that you and Lane are together again I can't see her being very successful,' Enid proposed encouragingly.

Now that she and Lane were together again? Jenna half laughed hollowly to herself. Their only togetherness was that they lived under the same roof and ate at the same table! And as for Rosalind not fulfilling her ambitions, she knew that to be no more than a pipe-dream too. She may not have had the wedding ring she so obviously coveted, but she sure as hell had everything else! The knowledge only helped to crush Jenna's spirits further and she spent the rest of the day moping aimlessly about the house. After Rosalind's belittling remarks she could not even resurrect an interest in her knitting any more.

'Enid tells me you received a visit from Rosalind today,' Lane mentioned casually during dinner that evening.

'Yes,' Jenna shrugged as she toyed absently with the food on her plate. She had had very little appetite of late.

'And?' he probed, not quite so offhandedly now.

She pressed her lips together but did not look up. 'We talked for a while, that's all.'

'I wouldn't have thought the two of you had much in common to talk about,' he forwarded in wry accents.

'We don't.' Except for you, of course! 'So I expect that's why she didn't stay all that long.'

'She didn't by any chance say anything that upset you, did she?' he enquired watchfully after a time. 'I know she can be somewhat startlingly forthright at times.'

That was putting it mildly! Jenna raised her head, her smoky gaze holding his determinedly across the table. 'What could she possibly say that would be likely to upset me?' she countered. Her being in love with him was the only reason Rosalind's comments had hurt, but that was something she could never reveal. She was suffering enough just being in the same house with him, without providing him with that weapon to use against her as well!

'I just thought she may have . . .' He broke off, shaking his head. 'It doesn't matter. If she didn't worry you there's no point in discussing it.'

Jenna accepted his decision compliantly and returned her attention to her food. Rosalind Cornell was the last person she wanted to discuss, anyway. It only reminded her of the travesty of a life she was living!

The ensuing silence was broken again by Lane presently. 'Enid was also saying you rarely leave the house,' he relayed quietly. 'Is there any particular reason for that?'

Apart from his remoteness that was tearing her in two and destroying her interest in life in general, did he mean? 'I wouldn't want to be accused of being a social butterfly again,' she grimaced.

'There are other places to go besides parties, you know!' For the first time since she had moved in his voice lost some of its patient blandness.

'And very few of them enjoyable on your own!'

'So take a girl-friend or two with you.'

'They're all at work during the day,' she advised flatly.

Lane eyed her contemplatively for a second or two, then he exhaled ruefully and rubbed a hand around the back of his neck. 'Okay, it would appear I've been elected. So where would you like to go?'

'*You're* offering to accompany me?' Jenna could not hide her surprise, or to her dismay, her pleasure the idea engendered.

'Uh-huh,' he drawled lazily. 'Don't you think I should?'

All of a sudden she remembered him saying that his spending his working hours with her had been the cause of his firm's near downfall before, and the glow that had appeared in her eyes only moments before was abruptly extinguished.

'Not when I know you'd rather be at work,' she declared somberly.

'Where did you get that idea?'

She made an indefinite movement with her head. 'You said that was the reason the business suffered so badly before.'

'Mmm, but matters are somewhat different now. With the staff I've got these days I doubt that's likely to reoccur. In any event,' his mouth shaped lazily, 'you seem to have forgotten tomorrow's Saturday and work doesn't even come into it. So once again ... where would you like to go? To visit your parents, to see friends, for a drive, to the beach?'

'The beach,' she elected quickly, but with a strangely shy smile. It had always been a venue they both enjoyed, and although her waist had thickened a little and her usually flat stomach was now slightly curving, she was sure she still had a once-piece costume that would fit her.

He accepted her decision acquiescently. 'Any one in particular?'

'Well, I did read in the paper this morning that there'll be a Surf Carnival on tomorrow at Mona Vale,' she relayed diffidently, naming one of the many beaches that adorned the city's northern shoreline.

'Then Mona Vale it is,' Lane acceded with such indolent cooperativeness that it had her vainly speculating as to the reason for his sudden change in attitude during the remainder of the evening.

Once morning arrived, though, Jenna put all her musings behind her. She did not really care any more why he had altered, she was just happy that he had, and was determined to enjoy every minute she spent in his company in case the opportunity did not come her way again.

Their journey to the beach did not take long to accomplish and there was time for an energetic swim

and a considerably less active sunbathe before the
carnival got under way. Run by the Surf Life Saving
Association—a uniquely Australian institution wherein
all its voluntary members patrolled the nation's
beaches and guarded the swimmers' safety thereon
entirely without payment, in fact by having to pay a
subscription themselves, every such life-saver paid for
the privilege of risking their life for others—there were
teams there representing just about all the clubs from
both north and south of the harbour, as well as some
from interstate, to take part in the exciting spectacle
beneath a blazing sun.

The carnival consisted of a variety of events. Rescue
and resuscitation drills, swimming races, surf ski
races, iron man contests: which required competitors
to swim one hundred and twenty metres out to sea,
round half a dozen buoys, and back, then paddle a surf
board with their hands out and around more buoys set
an extra ten metres from shore, followed by paddling a
surf rescue ski a further fifteen metres out and back,
concluding with a seventy-five metre run along the
beach to the finish line, and all without a break
between! Beach sprints and relays, and perhaps the
most exciting of all, especially when such a heavy sea
was running, surf boat races. Today, two of the boats
overturned coming back through the foaming, crashing
waves and a couple of oars were snapped but,
fortunately, no one was injured. The march past of the
teams that had competed was a pageant of brown skins
and colourful traditional costumes, each team wearing
a different colour and design, their leaders carrying
large pennant flags in matching colours.

It was late in the afternoon before it finally finished
and Jenna was drowsily content during the drive

home. The time spent with her husband had been all she had hoped it would be, and she felt happier than she had for some time.

'The day appears to have agreed with you,' Lane mused on flicking her a brief glance and noting her relaxed features, the darker golden complexion of her skin, the even brighter blonde streaks in her hair. 'Perhaps we should do it more often.'

Nothing would have pleased her more. 'Could we?' she queried half tentatively, half eagerly.

Once again his eyes skimmed over her, their expression unfathomable. 'You'd like to?'

Jenna nodded. Too nervous to speak in case the undisguisable enthusiasm she was certain would be evident in her voice, would reveal just how much she wanted to; but more importantly, why! Oddly enough in view of the circumstances that had brought them together again, she realised she probably loved him more now than she had when they were first married. Or maybe those years of separation had just brought a new depth, a new meaning to her feelings, but which in spite of his charming indulgence today, her pride demanded she keep hidden knowing they were not reciprocated any more.

'Right, then where shall we make for tomorrow?' he asked.

'I don't mind,' she owned with a smile. In truth she had not expected it to be so soon. 'Why don't you choose?'

His head tilted consideringly. 'Okay. How about a drive along the Great North Road and a barbecue in the bush?'

'The Great North Road?' she repeated, puzzled. 'I don't think I've even heard of it.'

'No, it's surprising the number of people who haven't,' he grinned. 'But it's the original convict-built road to Newcastle. Actually, after all the back-breaking work the poor devils put in to build it, it was only in use for about fifty years before a new route was surveyed—by all accounts it was hard going even on horseback—but it's still there in its original condition, hand cut sandstone blocks and all, and quite traversable, particularly in a four-wheel-drive. There's also a number of Aboriginal rock carvings and spear-sharpening stones in the area too that make interesting viewing.'

'You've sold me,' she smiled. 'Although it sounds as if it will be a very full day.'

'Which means, of course, we'll have to get an early start.' He sent her a wryly bantering glance. 'Do you reckon you'll be able to make it?'

'I'll make it,' she promised, drily decisive. If it meant another day like today, she would go without sleep altogether if necessary.

When the unexpected, but wholly satisfying week-end concluded Jenna expected her period of Lane's company to come to an end too, but to her astonishment, and consequential pleasure, it did not, because on the Monday he suggested they spend the day on the harbour in his launch and she agreed without reservation.

It was a lazy day as they desultorily explored the many sandy coves and inlets, some with thought-provoking names such as Quaker's Hat, Powder Hulk, and Sugarloaf Bays. They even tried their hand at fishing on one occasion when they came across a school of leatherjackets, and when their efforts were successful, exchanged the lunch of cold chicken that

Enid had packed for them, for one of fresh fish instead, which Jenna prepared in the boat's compact galley. It was not until they tied the launch up at the jetty below the house late in the afternoon that the atmosphere between them deteriorated abruptly, and then because she impulsively threw her arms around Lane's lithe waist and thanked him for such an enjoyable three days.

'I'm not interested in your gratitude, just a healthy child,' he rebuffed roughly as he purposefully removed her slender arms. 'It wasn't good for either of you to be inside so much.'

'I see,' she acknowledged in a tremulous voice and turned to pick up her bag so as to hide her suspiciously bright eyes. 'I'm sorry.'

When she came upright again her head was defensively high, but she made certain she jumped nimbly on to the jetty without his assistance. So it had all been for the sake of the baby, she grieved forlornly as she continued up the steps to the house on legs only a little less shaky than her voice had been. She should have realised his change of behaviour had not had anything to do with her personally. After all, he had made it plain enough just how he felt about her presence for some time now.

Feeling too distraught to face Lane for dinner that evening in anything even remotely resembling a composed state, Jenna made an excuse to miss the meal entirely and remained in her room until some hours had passed, and then left it only in order to make herself a hot drink. Actually, she had hoped to find the kitchen deserted by then, but as it happened Enid was still there, busily mixing a cake.

'I kept some dinner for you if you feel more like

eating now,' the older woman advised in a kindly tone on seeing who had entered. 'It won't take me a minute to get it ready for you.'

Jenna shook her head listlessly. 'No, thanks, Enid, don't bother,' she refused the offer quietly. 'I only came to make myself a drink.' And extracting a mug from a cupboard she filled it with milk before placing it in the microwave oven sitting on the bench top and switching it to the right setting. 'Where's Lane?' The words seemed to slip out without conscious volition. 'I couldn't see the office light on as I passed.'

Enid's mouth pursed and she added a few more ingredients to the mixer before replying. 'Miss Cornell rang shortly after dinner and he's gone to see her,' she relayed in an expressionless tone.

Nodding, Jenna pressed her lips together tightly, but could not prevent welling tears from entering her eyes. It did not really require a comment, but feeling something had to be said, decided on the matter that had niggled at her subconscious ever since her first meeting with the housekeeper.

'You knew Lane and I were married right from the beginning, didn't you, Enid?' she queried pensively.

Enid shrugged, half smiling. 'Well, since I knew his wife's name was Jenna—which isn't particularly common—I must admit I suspected as much, and especially in view of his attitude towards you.'

The bell on the microwave advised that her drink was ready and removing the mug Jenna spooned sugar into it and stirred it meditatively. 'I thought it may have been something like that.'

'For my being distant and reserved, you mean?' the other woman was not averse to putting it bluntly into words. 'Yes, well, I suppose having found Lane to be such an easy and considerate boss myself, I did tend to automatically assume that you must have been in the wrong where your marriage break-up was concerned . . . and for that I'm sorry. I realise there's more to it than that now.' She halted, her eyes resting on Jenna speculatively. 'And particularly in view of your present condition.'

A bitter, self-mocking laugh pushed past the knot of misery that was constricting Jenna's throat as she picked up her mug and began making for the door. 'The result of a mistake, pure and simple, Enid, I can assure you, and certainly not evidence of a reconciliation . . . as I'm sure you must have realised!'

'But—but the last few days!' the housekeeper exclaimed with a frown. 'I thought matters were improving between you at last.'

So had Jenna—fancifully, as it worked out. 'Mmm, but then our hopes rarely seem to come up to expectation, do they?' she countered sadly, and hurriedly departed before anything further could be said on the distressing subject.

Once within the privacy of her room again, however, Jenna left her drink untouched as she finally gave way to the tears that had been threatening ever since Lane had repulsed her spontaneous action. The knowledge that he was even now seeking his pleasure in Rosalind's arms making it impossible for her to deny them any longer as she sank down on to the bed and wept broken-heartedly.

When at last the rending sobs ceased she felt exhausted and dragging herself into the shower, she washed and made ready for bed spiritlessly. The moment her head touched the pillow, though, her tears started uncontrollably again, and they were still falling when she heard the slam of a car door some time later, followed shortly afterwards by slow footsteps mounting the stairs and then passing her room. Footsteps that unaccountably stopped and returned, and were succeeded by a rap on her door before it opened.

'Jenna, I'm sorry to wake you, but there's something I have to talk to you about,' Lane said heavily as he crossed the room towards the bed.

Huddling further beneath the sheet, she was glad she had her back to him so that the light streaming in from the hallway could not reveal her tear-stained countenance. 'It doesn't matter, I wasn't asleep, anyway,' she answered throatily.

Suddenly she felt the side of the mattress give as he sat on it. 'I'll be going away in the morning, and I don't expect to be back for a week,' he disclosed in the same weighty tones.

With Rosalind! she deduced with an involuntary shudder. 'All right,' she pushed out brokenly.

'There's something else too . . .'

She did not answer but lay waiting in a state of aching apprehension, and in the taut silence heard him expell an impatient sounding breath before the bedside lamp was abruptly switched on.

'Jenna, will you please turn round!' It was a direction, not a request, a forceful hand on her shoulder ensuring it was obeyed, and although she attempted to turn her head away she was prevented from doing so by relentless fingers spanning and immobilising her jaw. 'Oh, hell!' An expression of pain crossed Lane's face as he caught sight of her tear damp cheeks and wet, spiky lashes, and he rubbed at his forehead distractedly. 'I'm destroying you by making you stay here, aren't I?' he sighed. 'Maybe it would be best for all of us if you lived with your parents, after all.' He paused, drawing a deep breath. 'If you want to make the move while I'm gone, I won't stand in your way.'

So now he suggested it—after an evening spent with his girl-friend! Jenna observed resentfully, her desolation becoming tinged with a sustaining acrimony. 'Oh, I can do better than that!' she cried, snatching herself out of his hold and flinging back the sheet as she scrambled to leave the bed. 'I'll start packing now and that will get me out of your way even sooner!'

As unexpected as her move had been, Lane was equal to it and had grasped her arm and hauled her back to the centre of the bed before her feet could reach the floor. 'What the blazes are you talking about . . . in my way?' he demanded savagely. 'It's what you wanted, isn't it?'

'And when have you ever cared what I wanted?' she charged anguishedly, evading giving the answer he so obviously wished to hear. 'Why don't you just admit it's *you* who finds my presence unwelcome? At least your girl-friend was that honest.' The last came tonelessly.

'The . . .!' he smothered a furious expletive. 'I knew she must have been up to something when you said she'd been here!' His eyes blazed greenly as they locked with hers. 'And you believed her?'

'Why not? You made no secret of the number of times you visited her, or how you felt about her, and—and now you're just proving her right.' Her voice shook ungovernably.

'Because I said I wouldn't stand in your way if you wanted to·leave?' he countered tersely. 'But that's what you've always been after, isn't it?' And on an even harsher note when she averted her face, 'Well, isn't it?'

Jenna's lower lip trembled and her eyes blurred unbidden again. 'All right, since you evidently won't rest until you've made me say it, then the answer is yes!' she choked helplessly. 'Now you can continue your affair with the valued Miss Cornell with a clear conscience!'

'Damn bloody Miss Cornell!' he surprised her by cursing vehemently. 'I'm not interested in . . .' He came to a sudden halt, his gaze narrowing intently. 'And just why should I have to *make* you say it? I thought you'd be champing at the bit to do so.'

Realising her mistake, Jenna squirmed uncomfortably and made an effort to put more distance between them. 'As—as I said, so you c-could have a clear conscience by not being f-forced into telling me to—to leave yourself,' she parried falteringly.

'And why would you want to considerately present me with such a clear conscience, hmm?'

'Because I—because it . . . oh, just go away and leave me alone, Lane!' she ordered evasively, twisting away from him. 'You've got what you wanted! Isn't that enough?'

'No, it isn't! And particularly when I haven't got what I want at all!' he contradicted fiercely, and grasping her wrists dragged her inexorably back to him whereupon he pinioned them to the bed on either side of her head. 'Because if you must know, *this* is what I want!' His shapely mouth lowered to hers determinedly.

'No!' she protested despairingly, her head thrashing frantically from side to side, but to no avail.

His lips still captured hers unhesitatingly, the contact hard and over-powering, and immediately setting her heart to beating a wild tattoo against her ribs as her breathing became more and more ragged. Her senses were reeling and she sobbed hopelessly on knowing herself to be surrendering. She could not help it. The response he drew from her was uncontrollable, the sensuous quality of his kiss irresistible.

When he eventually released her, Lane's chest was rising and falling sharply. 'For God's sake, Jenna, do you think I would have insisted you live with me if I hadn't wanted you here?' he questioned hoarsely. 'It wasn't the baby so much as *you* I wanted!' He shook his head, uttering a ruefully self mocking laugh. 'It's only ever been you I've wanted.'

'A-apart from Rosalind, of course!' she gibed jerkily. Oh, if only she could believe him!

He moved his head slowly from side to side. 'Apart from no one,' he contended deeply. 'Oh, I admit our association wasn't purely business, but it was in the main—no matter what I at times, or she may have insinuated to the contrary—and . . .' his lips twisted wryly, 'I certainly wouldn't have bought a company solely in order to gain access to *her*, believe me!'

Jenna stared at him, her eyes widening incredulously. 'Are you saying . . .?'

'That I bought Hodgson Industries for the sole purpose of contacting you again?' he finished for her. 'Uh-huh!'

'But you couldn't have!' She gave a disclaiming shake of her head. 'You're far too hard-hearted in your business dealings to do something as unprofessional as that.'

'Except where you're concerned . . . as usual!' Lane said drily. 'And you tell me how else I was going to be able to get near you again otherwise. Any other approach and I doubt I would have reached first base.'

Her brain seemed incapable of taking it all in. 'But—but . . .'

A silencing finger was laid across her soft lips. 'I love you, Jenna!' Lane vowed huskily. 'And after the void your leaving made in my life last time, you'll never know what it cost me to offer you your freedom again tonight!'

Grey eyes gazed searchingly into hazel-green. 'You mean, you don't really want me to leave?' she still had to query on a tentative note.

'God, no!' His denial was adamantly unequivocal. 'I spent five long years without you, my love. If it's at all possible, I'd rather not add one single day more to that period.'

'Oh, Lane!' she breathed unsteadily as her arms, freed now, slid around his neck. 'Love me . . . please, just love me! After your rejection this afternoon, and then your seeing Rosalind tonight, I thought I'd lost you for ever and I just wanted to die! I need you, Lane, I always have! The same as I did when—when Kerryn died, only I was too proud to ask!'

'And I was too proud to offer!' he confessed in tones of self-castigation. Then cupping her face gently between his two hands. 'While as for loving you . . . believe me, I've never wanted to do anything else!' His lips, warm and vibrant, sought the sweet softness of hers again.

With no reason for restraint now, Jenna gave of herself spontaneously, her body moving against his pliantly, her hands slipping beneath the silk knit of his shirt to trace the smooth planes of his muscular back. Seeking the hollow of her throat with his tantalising mouth, Lane removed her nightdress swiftly, her breasts, already swelling due to her pregnancy, overflowing his cradling hands and throbbing under his exhilarating touch. An aching desire, clamouring for satisfaction, spread through her and she moaned helplessly, her slender form aroused to fever pitch and rising invitingly against his obviously no less stimulated frame. Their joining came quickly, their movements quickening compulsively as their rapture grew and each sought to please only the other, until at last they reached an exploding fulfilment that sent ripple upon ripple of wild sensation surging through Jenna, so that she felt intoxicated just by the ecstasy of it, and totally blissful.

'Now you know why you had to *make*. me say I wanted to leave,' she murmured shyly some minutes later as she lay with her head resting on a warm shoulder, Lane's arms encircling her securely. 'In spite of everything I still loved you too much to have left voluntarily.'

His hold on her tightened imperceptibly. 'You didn't appear so keen on the idea of living here originally.'

'Feeling as I did about you, I couldn't stand the thought of only being here on sufferance because of the baby,' she recalled sadly. 'And then after I had moved in, you were so cool and distant towards me—those times you were here, that is—that I just lost interest in life altogether, I guess.'

'If only I'd realised!' Lane sighed remorsefully. 'I attributed it to your hating being here, while the reason I absented myself so much was because I knew that if I didn't I wouldn't have been able to keep my hands off you, wanting you as I did.'

'So you kept visiting Rosalind instead,' she accused in reproachful accents.

'But only for business reasons,' he impressed decisively. 'Having had no business experience at all before her father died, she hadn't a clue how to run the company, and on most occasions it was only in an advisory capacity that I spent time with her.'

She was silent for a time, and then ... 'Although you *have* slept with her, haven't you?' she probed hesitantly, wistfully. The other girl could not have made the claims she had without at least some basis of truth in them, surely!

Lane exhaled heavily and, half turning towards her, brushed the back of his hand down her cheek, in a tender gesture. 'No, I've never slept with Rosalind,' he denied. His sensuous mouth slanted crookedly. 'I may have gone to bed with her, but I've never had the slightest desire to sleep with her.'

Jenna's eyes clouded pensively. 'Is there a difference?'

'To me there is,' he nodded resolutely. 'Going to bed with someone is merely a means for gaining a brief feeling of satisfaction, a moment's passion ... but to my mind, sleeping with someone,' pausing, he bent to kiss her meaningfully, 'is wanting to remain after the love-making, to hold them in your arms while you sleep, and the pleasure of knowing they'll be there in the morning. And that desire I've only ever experienced with you, my love.'

Reassured somewhat, Jenna pressed contentedly closer. 'Although you weren't there in the morning that last weekend I stayed here,' she still felt entitled to remind him. 'In fact, as I remember, you couldn't get to Rosalind's fast enough that day too.'

'Only because I couldn't trust myself not to want to make love to you again—you were nestled against me so very temptingly, my pet—that I considered it prudent to take my leave of you, no matter how reluctantly, while I still could.'

'And left me wishing you hadn't,' she confessed, sighing. 'You'd just made me realise you were still the only man I wanted in my life and I was looking forward to seeing you again, hoping to find you perhaps felt the same way too. Only you'd already left!' Her gaze turned admonishing again.

'I wouldn't have if I'd known, I can assure you!' he smiled with captivating eloquence. 'But considering how it had come about, I thought it more likely you would hate me for what happened.'

'Even though the second time I wasn't . . .' she ducked her head self-consciously, 'I wasn't exactly reluctant, is how you described it, I believe?'

'Even so,' he half-laughed wryly. 'Just because I'd managed to make you respond physically, unfortunately that was still no reason to assume I'd also managed to evoke any deeper emotion.'

'Idiot!' she charged lovingly. 'Do you really think I would have reacted quite so unreservedly if you hadn't?'

He laughed, and leaning over her tapped her beneath the chin with a long forefinger. 'Idiot yourself!' he grinned. 'For telling me there'd been no reason to inform your parents we'd met again, and thereby leading me to believe it meant you'd managed to get me out of your system, while I knew only too damned well I hadn't been able to do the same with you.'

Twin creases made an appearance between Jenna's brows. 'You mean, *that* was what caused such a sudden change in your attitude that night?' she gasped. 'I never could understand what had brought it about.' Abruptly, her eyes began to sparkle with humour. 'But for your information, the reason I didn't tell them was because I knew what their reaction would be. They always did think the world of you,' wrinkling her nose at him ruefully, 'and knowing just what a disturbing effect you were having on me anyway, I doubted their constantly lauding you would help put you out of my mind.'

'But thereby indirectly brought a new life into being,' Lane murmured, placing a hand tenderly on her gently curving stomach.

Covering his hand with one of her own, she smiled evocatively. 'Which you promptly claimed was Kent's.'

'You think I wanted to?' he countered expressively. 'But considering the way you kept implying you were having a heavy affair with the feller, you didn't exactly leave me with much choice, you know.'

'No, I suppose not.' Jenna bit at her lip regretfully. 'Although you're sure now, aren't you?' Her eyes lifted to his anxiously.

'Uh-huh!' he confirmed laconically, and perhaps because it was so succinct it seemed to carry more weight than a lengthier concurrence would have done. 'But while we're on the subject of Sharman . . .' his straight and glistening teeth suddenly showed in a lazy grin, 'that was quite a successful move sending him to Brisbane, wasn't it?'

Jenna glared at him mock-direfully. 'Because of his ensuing interest in someone else, or because it just enabled you to get him out of the way?'

'Both,' he laughed impenitently. 'I was tired of finding him with my wife every time I turned around, and I told you he wasn't right for you, anyway, didn't I?'

'Mmm, but then one could be forgiven for thinking that statement may have been just the tiniest bit prejudiced, couldn't they?' she quipped in mocking tones.

'Well, you must admit you *did* already have a husband, my love, and as it worked out, you could hardly call him faithful, now could you?' he drawled.

'You're a fine one to talk!' she promptly countered. 'At least I didn't have *his* girl-friend paying me an unwanted visit!'

'Don't remind me!' Lane's eyes rolled skywards expressively, his demeanour sobering. 'I had quite a few words to say to her about that, believe me, and despite your assertions to the contrary, I suspected she'd been doing her damnedest to drive an insurmountable wedge between us.'

'And probably would have succeeded if you hadn't ...' Stopping, she tilted her head to one side curiously. 'Is that what made you spend the last three days with me?'

'Among other things,' he owned drily.

'Such as?'

'Well, you obviously did need a change of scene, and ...' the curve of his mouth became ruefully pronounced, 'keeping your distance from someone is one hell of a strain when it's actually the last thing you want to do. So I figured it was time to try another tack—for my sake, at least.'

'And I loved every minute of it,' she smiled. Then added with an explicit grimace, 'That is, until I impulsively demonstrated my feelings this afternoon and was summarily rejected for my efforts!'

'Because I thought your action had been dictated by gratitude for having taken you out, and I wanted more, much more than that polite emotion from you,' he explained contritely, his voice thickening. 'Until then I'd managed to convince myself I could make do with just being near you, but when you threw your arms around me I knew it was hopeless, and I had to put you at arm's length somehow before I lost what little self control I did have left and responded in the manner every instinct was urging me to.'

'I see,' she nodded thoughtfully and proceeded to trail a finger slowly across his shoulder and down his sun bronzed arm. 'Although there's no call for you to show the same restraint now, is there?' She cast him a highly provoking glance from beneath long, curling lashes.

His acknowledging smile had her heart racing erratically. 'Lord knows how I managed to survive so long without you!' he groaned throatily as his lips found hers and his arms crushed her to him tightly.

After so many years of separation there was an urgent need to prove their love and it was some time before either of them spared another thought to conversation. When at last Jenna did, and her breathing had slowed a little, she gazed at her attractive husband adoringly.

'Do you really have to go away tomorrow?' she sighed.

'Only if you come with me,' he replied lazily, his fingers toying with the tousled strands of her hair. 'That was simply a plan to give me time to think things out. However . . .' he smiled at her indulgently, 'we could make it a second honeymoon if you like. To celebrate the start of our second marriage, as it were.'

'Mmm, I think I'd like that,' she breathed contentedly. 'Only this time . . .' she abruptly pushed herself up to eye him anxiously, 'we'll make a success of it, won't we?'

'Uh-huh!' Once again his laconic declaration was definite enough on its own not to require further strengthening.

'And I'll never leave this baby with a sitter!'

Lane sat up swiftly to clasp her by the shoulders. 'Jenna, that was an accident,' he insisted urgently. 'You weren't to blame! It was just one of those unfortunate mischances, that's all.'

'You said it was my fault at the time,' she half shrugged in a deprecating fashion.

'And I've regretted it ever since!' he divulged heavily. 'But as you may recall, things weren't exactly going well with us then, anyway, and . . .' his hands moved to cup her face and he smiled at her ruefully, 'did you mean everything *you* said at the time?'

Her eyes swam with sudden tears. 'No,' she whispered abjectly. 'But . . .'

Lane cut off her words effectively by kissing her, lingeringly. 'Then we'll leave all that in the past, where it belongs,' he directed softly as his head lifted. 'Okay?'

She nodded, and trying to recover her previous complacent mood, charged in a bantering tone, 'It didn't appear as if you'd forgotten the past when you first arrived at Hodgson's.'

The corners of his mouth swept upwards de-lightedly. 'That was in retaliation for your having deprived me of my wife, my love. Admittedly, for the first couple of years I kept telling myself I was better off without you, but no matter how hard I tried I just couldn't dismiss you from my thoughts entirely, and I eventually came to the conclusion that was simply because I didn't want you out of my thoughts, or my life.' He shook his head wryly. 'But, my God, did you have to make it so difficult to find you again? How was I to know you'd reverted to your maiden name?'

'You weren't supposed to,' she dimpled teasingly. 'And it was the only way I could convince myself I didn't still belong to you.'

'Is that so?' His eyes gleamed with feigned menace. 'And now?'

Jenna linked her arms about his neck, reaching up to brush his mouth lightly with her own. 'I know I always have belonged to you ... and I always will,' she murmured devoutly.

'The same as I've always belonged to you, and always will,' Lane repeated on a resonantly fervent note that left no room whatsoever for doubts.

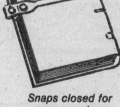

**Share the joys and sorrows
of real-life love with**

Harlequin American Romance!™.